He's gorgeous, powerful, successful.
Countless women have fallen for him.
But only one woman can tame him.
And she's about to discover what it's like to become
the bride of the sexiest tycoon on the planet....

Find out what happens
when a man who *always* gets what he wants
finally finds the woman of his dreams
in these two short, sparkling stories
from **Harlequin Romance®** stars

Patricia Thayer

The Tycoon's Marriage Bid

and

Liz Fielding

Chosen as the Sheikh's Wife

in

Becoming the Tycoon's Bride

Praise for Patricia Thayer

"Ms. Thayer leaves no emotion untapped
as her multifaceted characters make you laugh,
cry and get burned by the passionate heat
of true love. Keep the tissues handy!"
—*RT Book Reviews*

Praise for Liz Fielding

"*The Secret Life of Lady Gabriella*
is without a shadow of a doubt one of the
year's best category romances! Liz Fielding
has written an outstanding romantic tale that's
unmissable, unforgettable and unputdownable!"
—*www.Cataromance.com*

PATRICIA THAYER
LIZ FIELDING

Becoming the Tycoon's Bride

TORONTO • NEW YORK • LONDON
AMSTERDAM • PARIS • SYDNEY • HAMBURG
STOCKHOLM • ATHENS • TOKYO • MILAN • MADRID
PRAGUE • WARSAW • BUDAPEST • AUCKLAND

ISBN-13: 978-0-373-17715-8

BECOMING THE TYCOON'S BRIDE

First North American Publication 2011

This edition published by arrangement with Harlequin Books S.A.

For questions and comments about the quality of this book please contact us at Customer_eCare@Harlequin.ca.

www.eHarlequin.com

Printed in U.S.A.

PATRICIA THAYER

The Tycoon's Marriage Bid

Patricia Thayer has been writing for more than twenty years and has published thirty books with Silhouette Books and Harlequin Romance. Her books have been twice nominated for the National Readers' Choice Award, the Book Buyers' Best and a prestigious RITA® Award. In 1997 *Nothing Short of a Miracle* won the *RT Book Reviews* Reviewers' Choice Award for Best Special Edition.

Thanks to the understanding men in her life—her husband of more than thirty-five years, Steve, and her three grown sons and three grandsons—Pat has been able to fulfill her dream of writing. Besides writing romance, she loves to travel, especially in the west, where she researches her books firsthand. You might find her on a ranch in Texas, or on a train to an old mining town in Colorado. Just so long as she can share it all with her favorite hero, Steve. She loves to hear from readers. You can write to her at P.O. Box 6251, Anaheim, CA 92816-0251, or check her website at www.patriciathayer.com for upcoming books.

CHAPTER ONE

"YOU'VE got four weeks…but I want this deal wrapped up in two."

Hugh McCutcheon held the cellphone to his ear, listening to his father's orders as he drove his rental car along Interstate 5, just outside Medford, Oregon.

Why should he be surprised at the request? Whatever he'd done for the company, Richard "Mac" McCutcheon wanted more. "I thought Flanagan hadn't decided to sell…yet."

"And since when has that mattered to you?" his father asked. "I'm expecting you to come through for me. We need the orchard to control the area. More importantly, we need the vineyard."

Hugh should be used to getting this treatment from his father. *If the job's tough, give it to the kid. He'll do anything the old man dangles in front of his face.*

"I can't make any promises, Mac." It had been agreed he wouldn't call him Dad during working hours…that meant all the time.

"I don't need promises," he growled. "I need results. There's a lot riding on this, Hugh. Including the regional director's job."

Hugh sighed. *Yeah, right.* He'd been promised the position for the last year. "I'll do what I can. I need to go; my turn-off is coming up. I'll check in later." He shut the phone and tossed it on the passenger seat, next to the proposal for this project: Emerald Vale Orchard and Irish Rogue Vineyard.

On his flight from San Francisco to Medford he'd been able to scan it over, but not much more. His father wanted a lot, but he always had. Problem was the family patriarch, Cullan Flanagan, wasn't eager to sell his family business. The one positive thing was that the owner was giving the McCutcheon Corporation the opportunity to come and talk with him.

Hugh rubbed his hand over his face. He hated not being prepared for a job. In most cases he was always organized. But he'd just finished a six-week stay in Atlanta, where he'd downsized a recently purchased electronic parts plant. By the time he'd left the company was running efficiently, with a twenty percent reduction in personnel. That was sure to raise the next quarterly profit. It was important that he increase his value at the McCutcheon Corporation, too.

Hugh wanted that promotion…and he had that much of his father in him to ensure that he went after it. He'd gotten used to his lavish lifestyle. More than that, he enjoyed the thrill of his job.

So bring on the next challenge. He looked up to see the sign overhead: "Emerald Vale Orchard, est. by the Flanagan family in 1908. Home to the Irish Rogue Vineyard, est. 2002." He drove through the archway to see neat rows of pear trees along the hillside. On the other side were the ribbons of trellised vines.

Hugh continued on about a quarter of a mile and spotted a large barn, painted white with burgundy trim. In the front was a general store. He pulled up in the parking area next to picnic tables shaded by colorful shade umbrellas.

After climbing out of the car, he slipped on his suit coat. He glanced further up a grassy knoll to see a huge house with a flagstone façade that peeked out through the trees. A wraparound porch held baskets of summer flowers along the gingerbread trim. The manicured lawn was edged with more pink and purple plants.

Then suddenly the colors seemed to fade as a young woman stepped out onto the porch. What he noticed first was her rich auburn hair. The thick tresses went well past her shoulders and were clipped back from her face. She had a slender build. His gaze moved over her figure. A cream-colored blouse was knotted at her tiny waist, and her long legs were nearly covered by a gauzy peach-hued skirt. She moved gracefully as she lovingly attended to each plant.

He found his breathing suddenly labored, but his gaze didn't waver from the sight.

"The lass is easy on the eye, that's for sure."

Hugh jerked around to see a smiling older man in his seventies. He had a head full of thick white hair, and his face was weathered from years in the sun. Cullan Flanagan.

"I apologize for staring, sir," Hugh said.

The man's smile widened. "No need to apologize for appreciating a beautiful woman." He nodded in her direction. "I did the same thing the day I first saw her grandmother. And I felt the same way for the next fifty-three years." He sighed and blinked his eyes rapidly. "Sorry, I still miss her. And seeing Ellie every day brings back so many memories." He stuck out his hand. "I'm Cullan Flanagan. Welcome to Emerald Vale."

"Hello, Mr. Flanagan. I'm Hugh McCutcheon from the McCutcheon Corporation."

"Ah, Mr. McCutcheon, I've been expecting you." He looked him over. "So you think you can convince me to sell my land?"

Hugh gave him his best smile. "I plan to give it a try."

"It's going to have to be over my dead body," a woman's voice said.

Hugh swung around to see the redhead standing there, with her hands on her hips, glaring at him with large green eyes. She was even more beautiful close up. And he couldn't seem to find his voice.

* * *

Ellie wasn't going to let some big-city corporate guy come in here and take away her home. Not as long as she had any fight left in her.

"At a loss for words, Mr. McCutcheon?"

He shook his head, then smiled. "I assure you, Ms. Flanagan, I do not want any dead bodies."

"Oh, really?" She managed to look away from his dark chocolate eyes. "That's not what your reputation states. Don't they call you the Hatchet Man?"

He grimaced. "This business can be tough, especially when the companies we acquire are in financial trouble."

"Well, I guess you aren't needed here, since there isn't anything wrong with our orchard or our vineyard."

Hugh McCutcheon seemed to relax a little as he folded his arms across his massive chest, looking comfortable in his suit coat even when the temperature was in the high eighties.

Ellie didn't like that.

She didn't like men who walked in and acted as if they owned the place already. Well, no matter how handsome or well-built the man was, he wasn't going to take Flanagan land.

"Studies show there's always room for improvement."

"We're not a study, Mr. McCutcheon. We're a family and this is our livelihood. So go buy up someone else's place. We're not for sale."

"Eleanor Anne..." Her grandfather's voice broke in. "That's no way to talk to a guest."

Ellie turned to her sole grandparent. "It's true, Papa. Word has spread throughout the valley." She nodded to the stranger. "His company is buying up all the family orchards in the area."

"They were all willing to sell," Hugh added. "We didn't coerce anyone. We gave fair market value for all the properties."

Ellie made a huffing sound. "I doubt that," she said. "No one gets paid for all the years they've worked the land." She pointed toward the orchard. "Their blood, sweat and tears are out there. You can't put a price on that."

"I agree. But the owners who sold to us were ready to get out."

Silently, Ellie glared at him. She wasn't getting anywhere with the man, but she was more worried about her grandfather. Since the death of his wife Eleanor, two years ago, he'd been so unhappy. Nothing gave him joy anymore. Not even the winemaking. Something they'd planned and worked on together. The Irish Rogue label had been their collaborative dream. Now he was thinking about selling out.

Hugh knew Ellie Flanagan was going to do everything in her power to stop this sale. And his job was to do whatever it took to stop her. From what he'd read about the orchard, Cullan Flanagan was the sole owner of the land…and Ellie was his only heir. But she didn't have any control until after her grandfather's death.

"Maybe your grandfather is ready, too."

This time she couldn't hide her disdain. "He is not." She turned to the older man. "Papa, you can't be serious?"

"Can't hurt to hear what the man has to say."

Before Ellie could speak, Cullan raised his hand. "We'll discuss this later, lass. Please show Mr. McCutcheon to the Sunset Cottage."

She blinked those big emerald eyes, but quickly masked her anger once again. "Fine."

Cullan kissed his granddaughter, then looked at Hugh. "Please, make yourself comfortable, and I'll see you at dinner."

"Thank you, sir."

With a nod, the older man, his back bent slightly, his steps slow, walked across the gravel road toward the orchard.

"Just because he's invited you to stay doesn't mean he's going to sell you…all this," Ellie said, and she spread her arms, taking in the acres of lush green vines that led all the way up the hillside. On the other side were the rows of pear trees, dotted with the dozen workers who cared for them.

Hugh sighed. "I have to say, it's pretty impressive."

She drew a breath, too. "And it belongs to the Flanagan family. And I will make sure it always belongs to us."

"You have a big job ahead of you. Especially since there aren't many Flanagans left."

She straightened. "You don't need to worry about us, Mr. McCutcheon. Besides, who's to say I don't have a would-be husband around?" she tossed out. "Now, take your car down the road to the turn-off with the sign that says 'Cottages'. I'll meet you there." She took off toward the house.

Hugh enjoyed watching her walk away…too much. He wondered if there *was* a man in her life. She was beautiful enough to have several.

He quickly shook away the thought, and knew he'd better be able to handle a spitfire. "*Damn.* Keep your head on business. This trip is all about the business," he chanted, but the nudge of attraction didn't go away.

Ellie waited at the oak door to the studio cottage. The bungalow was usually rented by newlyweds, or couples who wanted the seclusion the peaceful orchard offered them. Not businessmen who wanted to rip her life apart.

The luxury rental car pulled up under the tree in front, and McCutcheon climbed out. He'd removed his suit jacket, revealing a crisp white shirt that showed off his broad shoulders and well-developed chest. Her gaze lowered to his trim waist, then, when he turned to walk to the car's trunk, she got a glimpse at his tight rear end. She quickly glanced away, angry that she could find anything to appreciate about the man.

With a dark leather suitcase in hand, Hugh McCutcheon walked toward her. Without comment, she opened the door and went inside. The combined scents of roses and peaches teased her nose as she stepped into the large room. As expected, there were fresh-cut flowers on the table. On the kitchen counter was a large bowl of fruit, along with several bottles of Irish Rogue wine. Soft music filtered into the space from strategically placed speakers.

There was a cozy seating area in front of the fireplace, and across the large room was a king-size bed covered in ivory satin, with miles of sheer fabric draped overhead, creating a canopy.

Definitely a place for lovers.

She looked at Hugh McCutcheon and noted his amused look. "I guess you don't have many singles, huh?" He loosened his tie as if he were too warm. She watched as he undid the top two buttons of his shirt, revealing dark chest hair.

She swallowed and turned to the phone on the table. "Sorry, we don't have the rooms equipped for Internet use."

This time he turned a wicked grin toward her. "I doubt that anyone staying here is thinking about business."

"No, not usually. Most of our guests have other things on their minds."

His gaze never left hers. "There are a lot of nice things to distract you here."

Silence hung between them as the music changed to an enchanting love song. The singer's sultry voice created an even more intimate feeling in the room.

Ellie froze under the man's gaze. She felt a sudden stirring low in her stomach. She swallowed, finding her mouth bone-dry. She blinked and finally broke the hold.

"If you need anything, Mr. McCutcheon, just call the office." She backed up, but came in contact with the coffee table and began to stumble.

Hugh reached out and grabbed her, pulling her upright. His hands gripped her arms, holding her firmly.

"You should be more careful," he said, his voice low and husky. "You could hurt yourself."

She nodded, not trusting her voice as her gaze locked with his once again. His brown eyes were incredible. Close up, they were the color of aged whiskey.

She glanced away, silently berating herself for her crazy behavior. This man was the enemy. He was here to take away her hopes and dreams. Straightening, she pulled away from his hold.

"I'm always careful, Mr. McCutcheon. I know what I want, and I'll do everything I can to keep what's mine."

He smiled. "Is that a threat, Ms Flanagan?"

"No. Just the truth. This land has been in our family for a hundred years, and I'm not about to let someone come in and take it away."

Hugh stood back and looked her over. Man, she was a powerhouse. Under other circumstances he would love to get to know her better. He pushed aside any thoughts of what might have been a passionate relationship. This was business—and business always came first.

"Times change, Ms Flanagan. It takes money to run an operation like this."

"We've been running it just fine for years."

"But at a profit?"

Hugh saw a flash of sadness in those mesmerizing eyes, but she quickly masked it. "Not everything is measured in dollars. And just because my grandfather and I are the only ones with the Flanagan name, it doesn't mean we don't have plenty of family around."

She gave him a once-over look that made him feel as if she could see inside his dark soul.

"I doubt you could say the same thing, Mr. McCutcheon." She swung around and walked to the door.

Hugh was just a bit quicker as he went after her. She reached for the knob, but he stopped her from making a grand exit.

"You know nothing about me, Ellie Flanagan…or my family." He spoke softly into her ear. "So don't go making assumptions. I'm not doing anything illegal, but I will do what it takes to get end results."

She turned around and flashed those big eyes at him. His gaze moved to her hair, already teasing his nose with a fresh lemony scent. He itched to run his fingers through the silky auburn strands.

"Then be warned, Mr. McCutcheon. I can fight dirty, too."

He couldn't help but smile as he stepped back. "I'll look forward to it."

She nodded, then pulled open the door and stalked out.

Hugh stood in the doorway and watched as she walked down the hill toward the house. With her head held high, her natural grace drew his interest more than it should. He wanted to blame it on a lack of female attention due to his heavy work schedule, but he knew the sassy redhead intrigued him all on her own.

If he allowed it, Ellie Flanagan could make him forget every other woman he'd ever known. She could also make him forget the reason he was here.

He frowned. No, he couldn't let that happen.

CHAPTER TWO

Two hours later, Hugh leaned back in his chair in the Flanagans' dining room. He glanced at the sage-green walls with a honey oak trim, and at the teardrop chandelier hung overhead. He took a sip of his wine, savoring the fruity taste.

"The meal was delicious, Ellie," he told her.

"Thank you," she answered, although she didn't look too happy with his compliment.

Cullan Flanagan smiled. "My granddaughter has many talents. She manages the vineyard and schedules all Eleanor's Special Events, then at the end of the day serves up a tasty meal."

"Papa, throwing together a stew isn't a difficult task."

"And homemade biscuits," he added.

"Well, it sure was a treat for me," Hugh said, meaning it. "I usually eat in restaurants while I'm on business trips."

"You travel a lot?" Cullan asked.

"More than I'd like," he conceded, wondering when he had ever loved it. He'd been supposed to get some time off now, but Mac had other plans.

"So your home is in San Francisco?"

He nodded. "But I'm sorry to say I don't have much time to enjoy the city."

Cullan sighed. "That has to be hard on your family, you being away so much."

"Then I guess it's a good thing I'm single."

"It can be a lonely existence."

"Maybe some people like the single life," Ellie added as she got up from the table and retrieved the coffeepot from the antique sideboard. She leaned close to Hugh to refill his cup and he inhaled her fresh scent. The sudden feeling of awareness caught him off guard.

He quickly looked back at Cullan. "There is my father, but he works just as much as I do."

The older man smiled. "I've talked with…Mac. He speaks highly of you. You must have a close relationship."

Hugh stole a glance at Ellie. She sat quietly, drinking her coffee. Suddenly he felt like a kid again, making excuses for his father's lack of attention. "Like I said, I don't have much personal time."

"That's a shame," Cullan said. "I don't know what I'd do if I didn't have my Ellie here with me."

"And I love living here, Papa." She reached over and gripped a gnarled hand that showed his years of working the earth. The love they shared was obvious.

Her grandfather looked sad. "Sometimes I wonder what kind of life it's been for you, lass."

Ellie smiled at him. "Papa, you've given me everything." She glanced at Hugh. "This land is important to me…I love managing the vineyard."

"It's been her life since she came home from college," Cullan said, then turned to his granddaughter. "You don't even think about a husband?"

A soft blush rose over her cheeks. "Why should I go looking for someone when you've never approved of anyone I've brought home?"

Hugh suddenly felt jealous of every one of those men.

Cullan waved his hand. "None of those fellows were worth your time. None of them loved the vines…not as you do. You need someone strong, someone who will let you follow your heart."

"My heart is just fine, Papa."

Cullan grinned as he looked at Hugh. "She is stubborn. All I want is to see her happy and to have a chance to play with a great-grandchild before I leave this earth. Is that too much to ask?"

Hugh raised a hand as he looked at the beautiful woman… who no doubt would give a man beautiful babies. "I think I should stay out of this."

"Good idea," Ellie agreed, then eyed her grandfather. "Papa, it will be a long time before you go anywhere. So stop talking foolish."

Ellie hated that her grandfather had brought up this issue, especially in front of a stranger. Had that been the reason he'd been entertaining the idea of selling the orchard and vineyard?

"See, she puts me in my place," her grandfather said. "Is it any wonder that men go running?"

"She hasn't scared me off," Hugh said.

That brought a big grin from Cullan Flanagan. "I knew I liked you. Now, I'm going to retire for the night." He stood and went to kiss Ellie. "I hope your accommodation is satisfactory, Hugh."

"Yes, it is. The cottage is very comfortable."

Flanagan nodded. "Then I will see you both in the morning." He walked out of the room.

The last thing Ellie wanted was to be left alone with Hugh McCutcheon, but she saw her grandfather's fatigue and knew he needed sleep. She turned back to Hugh and began to stack plates. "You should probably turn in, too."

"It's early yet." He, too, gathered up some dishes, followed her into the oversized country kitchen, then placed them on the counter.

"Thank you," she said.

When he returned to the dining room for more dishes, she spoke up. "You really should turn in. We get up at dawn around here."

"I will. After I help you clean up."

"You're a guest here."

"I'm a businessman, and your grandfather was nice enough to invite me to supper." He leaned against the counter and after a while said, "I know you don't want me here…"

"How observant of you, Mr. McCutcheon."

"Please, could you at least call me Hugh?"

"Maybe." She began placing the plates in the dishwasher. "But then why would I want to get too friendly with someone who wants to take away my business?"

"I'm not taking away anything. I'm making an offer. Your grandfather is the one who decides to sell or not."

The last of the dishes were put in and she shut the door. "Okay, it's done. Thank you. I'll say goodnight now." She started to walk away. Anything to get far from this man.

He reached for her hand and stopped her. "Please, it's early yet," he told her. "Why not give me a tour through the vineyard?"

She tried not to be distracted by the warm tingle caused by his touch, but couldn't hide her surprise at his request. "And why would I want to do that?"

"To show me why this place is so important to you. I've read a lot, but my knowledge is limited when it comes to orchards… or growing grapes."

The last thing Ellie wanted to do was help in any way to promote this possible sale, but Hugh McCutcheon wasn't going away anytime soon. Not until he was ready. So what would it hurt?

"Fine, I'll take you." She headed for the back door. Grabbing a sweater off the hook, she went out to the porch, not waiting to see if he was following.

"Hey, wait up. I didn't know this was a race."

Ellie stopped and swung around, only to collide with him. Immediately she raised her hands to regain her balance, and felt his hard body beneath his starched shirt. But when his hands gripped her arms she felt gentleness, too.

In the moonlight, she saw the shadow of his handsome face. She couldn't see his eyes, but felt his piercing gaze.

"You should be more careful," he said, his voice husky. "There isn't much light out here."

His warm breath brushed against her face, causing her heart to pound in her chest. She needed to step back, but couldn't seem to move. "I've been running through this orchard day and night since I was a child."

As much as he hated to, Hugh let her go. "You must have had quite a childhood."

They walked across the narrow farm road and through an open gate to the vineyard, and started down an aisle of grapevines woven along trellises. "To my parents' dismay," she began, "Papa and Nana spoiled me. It made it difficult when we all lived here together."

He couldn't hide his surprise. "All in the same house?"

She shook her head, and that glorious, wild hair caressed her shoulders. "No. We lived in a smaller house on the other side of the hill." She pointed past the vineyard. "It was my father Daniel's dream to become a winemaker. He planted the first Chardonnay grapes here fifteen years ago."

Moonlight guided their journey through the neat rows of vines. The night was silent, with just the quiet sound of their footsteps against the packed earth. He felt peace come over him and he began to relax.

"Later, my father expanded the vineyard and planted Pinot Noir and Riesling grapes. He had planned to build his own winery…"

"What happened to those plans?"

She kept her head down. "He and my mother, Marianne, were killed in a private plane crash. It had been their first vacation in years…a second honeymoon."

"I'm sorry, Ellie."

She nodded and didn't say anything as they walked on. "I want to carry on my father's dream and build up the Irish Rogue Vineyard."

"And your grandfather has other ideas?"

She shrugged. "I wouldn't say that… It's just since Nana died two years ago, he hasn't been enthusiastic about much of anything."

"He seems happy enough now."

She stopped, then turned back down another aisle. "You wouldn't say that if you'd ever seen him with my grandmother. They had a special relationship. She'd walk into a room, and Papa's gaze would follow her everywhere. He was always touching her, making her feel special. Every day of their marriage he'd leave the orchard to come to the house for lunch. They shared everything, every decision…every hope and dream. Then she got sick and he couldn't help her…" She stopped, and he heard her swallow before she continued. "All Papa could do was stay with her until the end…then he had to let her go."

Hugh couldn't say anything. He'd never known anyone who'd had a good marriage. His father had had two, and his mother had become bitter over the divorce.

Ellie stopped and looked at him. "Nana asked me to watch out for him. I've tried, but he misses her so…" He could hear the tears in her voice. "That's why I wasn't surprised that he let you come here."

Hugh knew better than to get emotionally involved with a potential client. But Ellie made it hard to stay impartial. "Maybe Cullan is just tired of all the work?"

"He doesn't have to do a thing. I'm here. I'm handling the vineyard. And Grandfather has a manager, Ben Harrington, for the orchard." She paused. "But you already know this, don't you, Mr. McCutcheon?"

"Most of it was in the report."

She straightened. "So you needed me to fill in the rest? You wanted to find our weak points? Well, you're not going to get any more information from me." She stepped closer. "You can write this down, Mr. Hugh McCutcheon. I don't give up. Not when something this important is at stake."

"I wasn't trying to gather information, Ellie. I was just enjoying a relaxing walk and some conversation."

"Who are you kidding? You're not the type to relax…unless it's to your advantage. And if you think I'm going to make this easy on you, you're crazy. So if you want to take this land, be prepared for a fight. Just remember there's a hundred years of Flanagans who have been in this area. And I plan to carry on that tradition."

Hugh hadn't envisioned any of this, especially this beautiful adversary. "There's got to be a way to compromise," he suggested, but he knew his father had too much invested in this project already to back down.

"As far as I'm concerned there's only one way to do that. Get off my land. It's not for sale." She swung around and marched down the aisle toward the house.

Hugh sighed as he started back at a slower pace. This wasn't going to be easy to pull off, but he wasn't giving up either. That wasn't his style. He thought of his fiery-haired opponent with those sparkling green eyes.

It's not over, Ellie Flanagan. I'll win you over one way or the other. But he wondered if his thoughts had anything to do with business.

"How is it going, Hugh?" his father asked the next day.

Hugh wasn't ready to take a phone call from Mac, but he wasn't left any choice. "Cullan Flanagan has been agreeable, and is willing to show me around, but he could just be playing me. His granddaughter wants me off the property."

Mac made a snorting sound. "I expect you to handle *her* without any problem. Just charm her. It won't be the first time."

Hugh walked to the window of the cottage and looked over the vineyard, seeing workers tending the fields. He wasn't proud of it, but he had in the past used a little gentle persuasion on the ladies.

"Ellie Flanagan doesn't want me here," he emphasized again.

"Maybe you should reconsider and bring in Matt Hudson. It was his project originally."

"No, I want you to do this. Now, you can't let me down on this one, Hugh. You know what's at stake."

Of course he did. The regional director's position he had wanted for the past year. "I'll try, but if not, isn't there any way we can work around this section of land?"

"Whether there is or not isn't the question. I've already put in place a potential deal with a chain of discount stores who want to buy large quantities of Irish Rogue wine."

Hugh felt a twinge of regret, knowing that when his father wanted something, he found a way to get it. "I can't guarantee anything, Mac."

"Come on, son. Work some of your magic." With that, the phone connection was cut off.

He tossed the cellphone on the bed with a curse. Son. He'd called him son. Why hadn't the endearment meant more? Maybe because there were always strings attached to it.

How could he let this happen? How could he be talked into something that would possibly destroy a family? Of course he had personal experience of how much his father cared about family. All those years ago Richard McCutcheon had walked out on his wife and ten-year-old son without a backward glance.

In the years that had followed he'd given generously of his money, but had rarely had time to spend with his child. It hadn't been until Hugh had graduated from college that his father had finally acknowledged him. He had asked him to come and work for the company. Now he still seemed to be looking for the old man's acceptance. The way it looked, it was never going to happen.

A knock on the door brought him back from his daydreaming. He went to answer it and found Ellie Flanagan standing in the doorway. She had on snug-fitting jeans and a print blouse. A single braid hung down her back. Those green eyes twinkled with mischief.

A warm shiver went through him. “Good morning, Ms Flanagan. What can I do for you?”

“How would you like to take another trip through the vineyard, this time in the daylight?”

He could only manage a nod. She could lead him around and he'd follow her anywhere.

CHAPTER THREE

"THE lack of rain has actually been good for the grapes," Ellie said as she stood beside the Riesling vines. "Too much water and the grapes aren't concentrated enough, but too little and the fruit flavor suffers."

Hugh could see her enthusiasm and pride as she did her job as a vintner. She was definitely qualified, having studied Viticulture and Enology at the University Of California.

Ellie plucked a cluster of pale-green grapes, then walked back to the battered Jeep, where Hugh was leaning against the side. Surprising him, she held up a plump grape. Her eyes danced with mischief and challenge.

Suddenly he felt like Adam with Eve, and he couldn't deny her. He leaned forward and took the grape with his teeth, taking a teasing nibble from her finger. As the warm juices filled his mouth she pulled her hand back, a surprised look on her face, but she didn't move away from him.

He made a sound in his throat, but couldn't decide if it was because of the tart fruit, or because of the desire she stirred in him.

"It's very good," he managed, wondering if she was doing this on purpose. He shook away the thought and tried to concentrate on business.

Hugh glanced around the acres of vines that were less than a month from harvest. "Why doesn't Irish Rogue vineyard have its own winery?"

Ellie popped a grape into her mouth and sat on the bumper, not far from him. "Like I said last night, it was my father's dream…and now it's mine. After I came home from college, I presented the idea to my grandfather. He liked my plans, but then my grandmother took ill. Of course we both turned our full attention to her."

She sighed. "Nana was sick for nearly three years. And by the time she passed away it had turned out to be a costly illness. Worse, it took a lot out of my grandfather. He hasn't had the same joy from his work as he always had before…"

Hugh didn't say anything. He glanced at the woman next to him. Her hair was tied back, but still the summer breeze blew at some wayward strands. He caught her near-perfect profile, the long lashes, her delicate jawline. Her flawless skin was dusted with light freckles, and she had a full mouth that was so tempting he had to fight to keep from reaching out to touch her.

Damn, when had he gotten so soft? He looked away.

"So you've pretty much handled everything?"

She nodded. "I manage the vineyard, and even though we use an outside winery—the Blackford Winery—I still oversee the process of our label, Irish Rogue. The Blackford family have been friends and neighbors for years. Henry and my father planned to build a winery together, but it never happened…" She paused. "I'm lucky enough to get to work with Henry, so you can say I have my hand in everything, from beginning to end."

Ellie knew she'd already revealed a lot to this stranger. What would it hurt to tell him what was already public knowledge? She got up, walked away, then turned back around.

"But you've already investigated all that, haven't you? I also know that your company tried and failed to buy out the Blackford Winery." She smiled. "You can't always get what you want."

He folded his arms over his chest. "You have no idea what I want."

"So it's not true that your father is trying to buy up all the small vineyards to gain control of the valley?" She felt the anger building. "He'll probably just ignore that every grower's grapes have an individual, unique taste. Does he also plan to throw all the grapes together, and change their labels?"

"Please, give us some credit."

She didn't let up. "I bet you already have new buyers lined up. And they all want to buy in bulk."

"What's wrong with that?"

"You can't rush perfection. Wine takes time. It also takes time to enjoy…to savor."

"Is that why they say women are like fine wines?"

His voice had a husky quality, sending a warm shiver through her. This man was going to be the death of her…if she let him, standing there in his fitted jeans and boots, and a starched blue shirt. She had to fight to resist her attraction to him.

"Maybe you should answer that one," she told him. "I'm just a simple country girl. My only concern is producing the best wine," she said, knowing she had to change the direction of their conversation. "Would you like to see the orchard?"

"I would rather talk to you about staying on to work for the McCutcheon Corporation."

Her mouth gapped open. "Whoa…you act as though it's already a done deal." She glared at him. "It's not. Besides, why would I want to come and work for your company?"

"To make fine wines, of course."

"I don't believe your managers and I would have the same point of view on how to run things."

"I'm surprised you wouldn't jump at the chance to change our minds."

Ellie wished that were true. "Why? Have I changed yours?"

"In all fairness, Ellie, I haven't seen or heard anything from you to convince me that buying up the small wineries will ruin the quality of the product."

Hugh could see Ellie's anger when she climbed into the driver's seat. "I've told you, it's not a race. I guess that would clash with the big business mantra of 'time is money'?" She started the engine. "I can't picture you sitting around and watching the grapes grow or age in oak barrels."

He grinned. "And that's the reason we need you. To teach us…to direct us." He grabbed the roll bar and climbed into the seat. She started the engine, jerked the vehicle into gear and took off.

Once out of the vineyard and on the dirt road, she picked up speed. They rode along in silence. He was about to start up a conversation, but thought better of it. He squinted into the sunlight. In the last twenty-four hours since he'd met her, Ellie Flanagan hadn't been any other way but straightforward and truthful. She was also beautiful, stubborn, and most of all protective of her family.

Oh, yes, she had to have the last word.

Just past the vineyard, she turned off again and drove along the bare strips of tire tracks in the grass. It was rough going as they rode through a grove of trees and along a rocky creek. She turned toward a shady spot under a large oak and parked. She jumped out of the vehicle and walked to the water, restlessly pacing back and forth.

"Okay, let's say my grandfather does sell this land to your company," she called out. "What responsibility will you take for our employees?"

He frowned, knowing he couldn't make any promises. "What do you mean?"

"The Flanagan family has employed a lot of workers over the years…sometimes entire families. They depend on the work. Will your company guarantee them jobs?"

He climbed out. "Ellie, you know I can't do that."

Her frown deepened. "That's what I thought. So your job is to cut the number of employees. We pick grapes by hand, but you'll probably change to machines."

Last night, Hugh had been reading up on the pros and cons of machine harvesting. "If it's more efficient, we would consider it."

She bit down on her lower lip and glanced at the creek, as if trying to come up with the right words.

"Look, Ellie. I know this possible change will be hard for you. But have you thought you could have everything you want without the headache? Your label, Irish Rogue, would still exist."

She gave him an incredulous look. "You still don't get it. This is our land. Flanagans have survived here for generations. My grandfather was born in that house," she said, pointing at the structure on the hill. "And my grandmother died here. She's buried here, alongside my father and mother."

Hugh could see her pain. "One of the stipulations your grandfather made was to keep the original small orchard and the house," he rushed to say. "So you wouldn't lose your home."

"Great. I'd have to watch someone else take over. It's not the same." She blinked rapidly.

Having lived in several places growing up, and his so-called family ties having been severed long ago, Hugh didn't understand the connection. But he wanted to, and maybe he was a little jealous she had such deep roots here.

He went to her. "Ellie…why don't you and I sit down with your grandfather—?"

She shook her head, then shot off up the hill. He went after her. When he reached the top of the rise, he found her in a fenced-off area surrounded by black wrought iron. He approached and saw several headstones. The family graveyard.

He stopped behind her. He didn't want to disturb her, but knew just his presence angered her. It had never bothered him before…he was just doing his job. But with Ellie it did.

They both looked down at the headstone for Eleanor Kathryn Flanagan. "She was more than my grandmother," she said, then drew a breath. "Nana stepped in when my parents died. She didn't even have time to grieve after losing her only son… because she had to deal with a teenager."

There were tears in her eyes as she turned and looked at

Hugh. His chest tightened, seeing her pain. He wanted so much to take her in his arms.

"It's a good thing she wasn't here when you arrived. She'd have run you off with a shotgun." Ellie managed a smile.

"I wish I could have met her."

"Oh, I don't know if you'd have liked that. Ask Papa. He'll tell you that Nana is who I inherited my temper and stubbornness from."

"At least you come with a warning." He reached out a tugged on her braid. "Your fiery red hair."

She tensed, but didn't pull away. "When I feel threatened… or think my family is…I fight back."

Hugh couldn't let go of the soft strands of hair. "You have nothing to fear from me, Ellie."

Her lips twitched. "Said the spider to the fly."

His heart raced. She was so beautiful, he didn't want to let her go. "Isn't it the female Black Widow that kills and eats the male?"

She continued to stand there. "You're the one who's not to be trusted."

"I've known a lot of females who can't be trusted also."

"I just bet you have."

"See, there you go, making assumptions. With all the traveling I do, I don't have time to meet many people…unless it's related to business."

"That's sad," she said. "You have no friends?"

"I didn't say that. I have friends, but I don't have much time to spend with them lately." He couldn't help but be curious about any man in her life. "What about you? Is your life consumed with the vineyard?"

She brushed a strand from her face as a warm breeze blew. "No, I have friends, too, and Papa…" She paused. "He doesn't go many places these days."

"He misses her, doesn't he?" Hugh nodded toward the headstone.

"Yes. I know that's the reason he talks about selling the vineyard."

"You ever think he also wants to secure a future for you, too, especially since you're single?"

"That's crazy." She stepped back. "I don't need a man to support me. I can go to work for any winery and make a good living." She was agitated now. "But I want this vineyard, the grapes that my father planted right here on Flanagan land. And soon I'll build our own winery," she stressed. "I know I can make it work."

Hugh believed her. Ellie Flanagan could do anything.

Two hours later, Hugh was back at the cottage. He was exhausted, and happy to get away from Ellie. He was starting to care about her…and Cullan Flanagan.

Mac's number one rule was: Don't get personally involved with people you do business with.

He was trying, but Ellie Flanagan had distracted him from the moment he'd laid eyes on her yesterday, and the last twenty-four hours hadn't diminished that.

His cellphone rang, and he knew who it was. Mac. He didn't like it when Hugh didn't call to report in.

He answered it. "Hello?"

"Well, it's about time you answered your phone. Where have you been all day?"

"Working."

"Are you making any headway?"

Hugh blew out a breath. "I've only been here a day."

There was a long pause. "At least tell me that you've been spending time with the old man."

No, his grand-daughter. Hugh walked to the large window and looked out at the vineyard, to spot Ellie talking with a worker. He wasn't close enough to see her face, but her body language revealed her enthusiasm. When she'd finished, she hurried off toward another destination, greeting other workers along her journey. She smiled and tossed her head, and laughed at something.

Hugh turned away. "No, Mac. I spent the day touring the land. It's quite an impressive operation. Did you know that his granddaughter has been planning to build a winery?"

"I've heard rumors, but it's not my concern. Your job is to get us this property."

"Maybe it should be your concern, Mac. The Flanagans aren't going to sell to us or to anyone. We're wasting time here."

"I wouldn't be too sure of that. I've done some research… Cullan Flanagan is in debt. Big debt."

Hugh had suspected as much. "So? A lot of businessmen take out loans."

"Flanagan had to take out a mortgage when his wife got sick. Her long illness was expensive, much of which wasn't covered by insurance. Cullan gave his wife anything and everything she needed, but none of it cured her."

Hugh was furious at his father's lack of compassion. "Some men love their wives enough to put them first."

"Okay, let's not stir up the past. What happened between your mother and me was a long time ago. It's water under the bridge."

Maybe for Mac it was, but Hugh could still hear his mother's sobs, and knew the pain his father had caused her. The pain that had transferred to the young boy who'd been abandoned, too. "So you're going to pounce when Flanagan's down and take advantage?"

"No, *you* are. Show me what kind of man you are. Make this deal happen."

CHAPTER FOUR

Make this deal happen.

Those words were still in Hugh's head the next morning, when he took off for a quick run to clear away his problems. If for just a little while.

Thanks to the help of the corporate secretary, Rita Copeland, he had plenty of information on the Flanagans, and he'd been awake half the night reading. Most of it was pretty boring. They'd had a few black sheep in the family over the last hundred years, but overall the Flanagans had been an asset to the community of Medford, Oregon.

If Mac had anything to do with it, they wouldn't be landowners much longer.

He turned his attention to the running path and took off toward the vineyard. The firm ground helped with traction as he made his way up the slight rise along the dirt road. There was a gray mist over the land, reminding him of mornings in the San Francisco area.

Here, the big difference was the wonderful silence. Even with workers tending the fields, there wasn't the sound of car horns or police sirens to disrupt his peace.

He'd covered about a half-mile when he spotted someone. With a second look, he discovered another runner. Picking up speed, he got close enough to see a woman in a tank top and shorts, exposing a lovely pair of long legs. His gaze moved up over the firm curve of her rounded bottom to the thick auburn braid bouncing against her back. Suddenly his breathing wasn't so controlled.

Great. So much for putting the woman out of his head.

As if she'd realized she wasn't alone, she turned around and tossed a frown.

It bothered him. "Funny to see you here," he said, pausing next to her.

"It's not funny at all," she told him. "Why are you following me?"

He tried to ignore the slight sheen on her skin, and her chest moving rapidly. He quickly looked away from temptation.

"I'm not following you," he stated. "I run all the time. I had no idea that you did, too."

She studied him for a moment. Her appraisal bothered him, causing his body to stir. Something he didn't need at the moment.

She stopped. "I think I'll head back."

"Wait, there isn't any need for that. Why can't we run together?"

"Oh, yeah. That'll be relaxing," she argued. "You with your endless questions."

He raised his hands in defense. "I don't talk when I run. I put all my energy into what I'm doing."

She rested her hands on her hips. "So you can't talk and walk at the same time?"

He chanced a smile, but didn't say anything.

When she began to walk again, he stepped in next to her. "How about we call a truce for now?" he suggested. "I'll only talk business during business hours." He glanced toward the east to see the sun just barely peeking over the horizon. "It's too early for business."

With her nod, Hugh let her pick the pace. Surprisingly, she was pretty fast. He liked that. He glanced at his running partner. Although she looked delicate, he suspected Ellie could hold her own in a lot of areas, or at least be stubborn enough to try.

"This is my favorite time of day," she said. "The cooling

mist…the clean smell of the earth and the air… I can almost feel the life in each vine…each cluster of fruit." Her arms pumped as she glanced at him. "Welcome to my world."

He was touched by her words. "Thanks for sharing it with me, Ellie." They continued on their run, not speaking again… but there was no need to.

That day, Ellie put all her energy into work, and stayed far away from Hugh McCutcheon. After he'd invaded her run, she had decided to avoid him. She didn't like how he'd managed to get her to forget why he was here, but somehow he had.

The next day she learned it hadn't been necessary, since Hugh had been holed up in the cottage for the past twenty-four hours.

No one had seen him.

And, as much as Ellie tried to concentrate on vineyard business, she couldn't stop wondering what the man was up to. Last night at supper, Papa hadn't given her any clues as to what he was planning to do, either. Not even a hint about selling the family business had been brought up during the conversation. Even if they'd talked about it many times before, she knew she couldn't change her grandfather's mind. Not if he truly wanted to take the McCutcheon offer. She knew her grandmother's illness and death had taken its toll on her grandfather. It was as if he'd given up.

Ellie walked through the vines toward the general store, recalling just weeks ago, when Papa had first come to her with the prospective deal. Even though the house and the original tiny orchard were held out of the deal, he was selling her heart… the vineyard.

She felt that was as much a part of her heritage as the house. If only she could buy the vineyard herself. But it would be impossible to get hold of that kind of money. Anger and sadness swept through her. She hated that there was a stranger here who could possibly take over. Why not someone local? Someone Papa respected and trusted?

Ellie stepped up onto the wood-planked porch and walked inside the general store. She smiled when she recognized some of the familiar customers mingling around. Many were locals from town.

"Hello, Ellie," one of the older ladies from the group greeted her.

Ellie recognized a customer, and shook her hand. "It's nice to see you again, Mrs. Powell."

The woman smiled. "We wouldn't miss the concert…and the wine, of course. And that nice man of yours said it should be a lovely night for it."

Suddenly Ellie remembered tonight was the weekly summer concert in the rose garden, *Good Wine and Good Music.*

"What man?"

"Hugh…Hugh McCutcheon." Mrs. Powell pointed toward the back of the store. "We were visiting the tasting room when he asked us some questions about the wine." Her smile widened. "He's a very polite young man…and handsome, too."

Ellie cursed Hugh silently. She hated the fact that he'd invaded all parts of her life. She kept her smile in place. "I should go make some preparations for tonight."

She excused herself and headed through the doorway in back that led into the tasting room. She glanced around the space, with its comfortable high counter and several stools. A huge built-in wine rack covered the wall behind, where several dozen bottles were laid on their sides.

Summertime usually brought in the tourists, and the weekly concerts increased that volume even more. Along with wine sales.

Ellie spotted Hugh at the counter, along with several other women. Why didn't that surprise her? Dressed in jeans and another starched oxford shirt, he was sampling wine. The young server, Jillian, was behind the counter, holding a bottle of reserve Irish Rogue Chardonnay, vintage 2004.

Ellie tensed. They usually didn't open the expensive wine

unless the buyer was a serious one. She needed to put a stop to this. The McCutcheon Corporation hadn't taken over yet.

Laughter rang out as she approached the group. Hugh turned to her, and his smile widened. "Ellie. We were wondering if you were going to be here."

"Since I run the place, it's a pretty good guess I would eventually show up."

Hugh could tell that Ellie was not pleased with him. What else was new? She hadn't liked him on first sight. He was curious to know if it was just because he was bidding on her property, or if it was more personal.

Funny thing was that he was beginning to care about this woman who'd run beside him yesterday at dawn. She'd shared her beloved land with him…along with a special part of herself.

"I've decided to take your advice and learn more about wine," he told her. "And I hear there's going to be a concert tonight."

Ellie glanced at Jillian, an attractive blond. She was a college student, home for the summer—and, according to her… available.

Hugh wasn't interested in anything more than sharing a conversation. He looked back at Ellie. Not with Jillian anyway.

"There's one every week during the summer," Ellie told him, flashing those incredible green eyes. "It was one of my grandmother's ideas."

"Well, it's a good one."

She seemed surprised at his compliment. "It's probably nothing compared to the concerts you have in San Francisco."

He stood. "If the music and company are good, you can't ask for anything more." He wouldn't have a problem sitting with her in the moonlight.

"You can't forget good wine," she added.

He smiled, and, surprisingly, she returned it. His pulse-rate sped up and he held up his glass. "And this is an excellent vintage," he told her. "But I should let you get back to work. I'll see you tonight."

With his wine purchase, Hugh walked out of the tasting room and back to the deck at his cottage. He didn't want to go inside yet. He'd been locked inside for the past twenty-four hours.

He placed his wine on the deck table outside the cottage and sat down. He needed to do some more cramming to catch up on this project—to learn about the Flanagans and the vineyard. The history of the place had fascinated him. There had been lean years and prosperous years over the decades for the family, and things right now looked bleak again.

And of course Mac McCutcheon had jumped at the opportunity. He'd stepped in and offered Cullan Flanagan several thousand dollars below market value for his land and his business.

Four years ago Cullan Flanagan had borrowed money to help offset the cost of his wife's illness. He'd never given a second thought to the consequences. Who would, when your wife needed treatment to stay alive? Even if it had only given Eleanor Flanagan another two years with her family.

Now it was going to cost Cullan. Everything. There was a balloon loan payment coming due in just a little over a month. Hugh seriously doubted Flanagan had the money to pay it. He'd already gotten one extension on the loan, and there wasn't going to be another. That was the reason Cullan had agreed to have a company representative come here.

Trouble was, Hugh doubted that Ellie knew all the facts about the deal he had come to offer. Did she have any idea that her grandfather was in over his head? Worse…that there was only one way out. To sell to the highest bidder. Right now that was the McCutcheon Corporation.

At dusk, Hugh's thoughts were still on Ellie as he made his way toward the back of the main house and the rose garden, where the concert was being held. Despite all warnings to stay clear of her, he looked forward to seeing her tonight.

He admitted he was drawn to her. He was quickly learning they weren't all that different, just because she lived in the country and he in the city. They had both grown up without the advantage of a traditional family. His parents had divorced, hers had died. They had both excelled in school and come back to work in the family business.

The bad side was, she saw him as the enemy. And she should. He was here to take her beloved vineyard.

"Why, Mac?" he breathed. "Why me?"

Hugh had done exceptionally well at his job of downsizing companies, but usually they were manufacturing businesses. It was all impersonal. But Emerald Vale wasn't just a building and machinery…or overpaid executives. It was a family. The employees were flesh-and-blood people.

Hugh strolled over the rise to see the stack-stone walls. A wrought-iron gate hung open, revealing a huge yard. He walked inside and found a beautiful haven. The stone walls were lined with rows of colorful tea roses. Slate stepping-stones were woven through the many floral bushes, along with several benches scattered around decorative water fountains.

On the lush green lawn were small round tables with chairs. Hurricane lanterns were lit, illuminating the intimate area. A jazz quartet were tuning their instruments from the platform.

Hugh had heard from some of the guests that the Flanagans' garden had been the backdrop for many weddings and parties over the past few years.

He searched the crowd of people taking their seats, hoping to find Ellie. Surely she would attend? Suddenly, he froze as she walked through the gate. She'd changed into a long print skirt and a fitted T-shirt, covered with a sheer cream blouse and a wide belt around her waist. Her hair was down, dancing around her face.

Smiling, she wove through the tables, stopping to talk with the guests. Taking a bottle of wine from a server, she began to fill glasses. He listened as she spoke about the vintage with knowledge…and pride. She was something. He'd never seen anyone have such passion about their work as Ellie Flanagan.

When the music started, Ellie moved back into the rose garden and stood as soft sounds filled the night air. She felt someone's presence and turned to find Hugh, holding out an empty glass.

"Haven't you had enough?" she whispered.

He grinned at her. "Not nearly enough…"

She felt a warm shiver race through her body. Somehow she managed to fill the glass.

He held up another glass. "Join me…please?"

She glanced at his face in the dimming light. She saw a look in his eyes that was both sexy…and dangerous.

She nodded, and, with his hand pressed against the small of her back, he guided her toward a vacant bench. Once they sat down the roses acted as a curtain, and the other guests were facing away from them.

The rhythm of the music was soft and sultry. Hugh sat next to her, but didn't talk. He seemed to relax as they listened to the quartet.

Ellie, on the other hand, was very aware of the man beside her. She closed her eyes and pushed everything out of her head as she tried to concentrate on the jazz. Instead she felt Hugh's heat, inhaled his musky scent… It was like a pheromone that seemed to heighten her awareness of the good-looking man. She moved restlessly in her seat.

Then there was a warm touch. Just the graze of his hand across hers. She should move it away, away from temptation, but she couldn't. Then his fingers laced through hers, and more heat spread through her.

The music swelled, as if cocooning them in their own private place…and time. She stopped breathing when Hugh raised her hand to his mouth and placed a kiss against the back. Another tingle rushed though her, and she jumped at the sensation.

"Ellie…it's okay."

She finally opened her eyes to see him leaning in. Her throat went bone-dry. "Hugh..." she managed his name.

He touched a finger against her mouth. "Don't talk. Let's just enjoy this," he whispered.

She drew a breath and recognized the raw hunger in those dark eyes. Not wanting to break the spell, she couldn't look away...or speak. But the decision was out of her hands as the music ended and the audience broke into applause.

Embarrassed that he'd managed to mesmerize her, she handed him her glass and picked up the bottle. "I need to get back to the guests." When he didn't stop her, she turned and walked away, wondering if he'd call her back.

The bigger question was, would she stay if he did?

"Is this your best offer?" Cullan asked Hugh two days later. They sat at the dining room table with the McCutcheon bid spread out in front of them.

Hugh wasn't sure what to say. There might be other bids, but he doubted it. "It's a fair offer...considering."

Cullan's gaze met his. His face was expressionless, but not his clear blue eyes. "If you got something to say, lad, you'd better say it."

Hugh sighed, wishing he was in a cold boardroom, with an overpaid executive. Not a man whose lined face revealed his years in the sun, whose hands were rough and crippled from hard, physical work. "I know you mortgaged the land... heavily."

"I figured your father probably knew that when he approached me a year ago about selling. Back then I told him thanks, but no thanks." The old man sighed. "I guess he just sat back and waited me out, figuring I wouldn't be able to make the loan payment."

Hugh tried to stay detached, but it wasn't working. "So you're going to sell the land?"

"Like you said, it's more valuable than the house and the

old orchard." The man suddenly looked years older. "Ellie's vineyard…"

"You'd better tell her. She already suspects something, but she needs to hear it from you."

"It's going to be hard to tell her I failed her."

"You didn't fail her, Cullan. Circumstances made it impossible for you to do anything else but take a loan against your property. You used the money for your wife, didn't you?"

Cullan just nodded.

"Ellie will understand when she knows the reason."

"I'm not so sure. I'm taking away her vineyard…her dream."

Hugh closed his eyes momentarily. "I can't make you sell to me, but you better do something fast—because you'll lose everything if you don't."

"Papa…"

They both looked up to find Ellie standing in the doorway of the dining room.

"Ellie," Cullan said as he got up and went to her. "I thought you went to the winery."

"I just got back." She glared at Hugh. "And it looks like not a moment too soon. Is this how you work, McCutcheon? Divide and conquer?"

"Ellie, please," her grandfather began. "We were talking business."

"Sounded more like coercion to me."

CHAPTER FIVE

ELLIE had returned from the winery and learned that Hugh and Papa had toured the orchard, then gone to the house. She'd hoped that it was just for coffee. The evidence on the table now, a contract for Emerald Vale, said otherwise.

"Papa…what's going on?"

Her grandfather glanced nervously at Hugh, then back to her. "Sit down, lass. I need to talk to you."

On stiff legs, she moved closer to the table. She didn't want to hear anymore…but she already knew what was coming. And it was going to be life-changing.

"I think I'll stand."

He stood slowly, using the table for support. "I'm going to sell to the McCutcheon Corporation."

She gasped. "No! You can't do that."

"I'd give anything if I had a choice…but I don't. I mortgaged the land when Nana was sick." She saw the pain etched on his face. "I can't pay it back."

The words echoed in her head over and over again. Still she didn't want to believe it.

"I'm sorry, Ellie. I wish it wasn't so, but there's no choice." A tear ran down her cheek as he came to her. "Please forgive me…"

Ellie wrapped her arms around the man who had loved and cherished her all her life. Who had tried to protect her from every bad thing.

"Oh, Papa. It's okay. You had to do it…for Nana. I just wish you had told me… I wish I could have carried part of the burden. Maybe I could have helped."

"It's too late…"

She forced a smile. "We have so much. We have each other. That's all that's important." She hugged him again.

Hugh walked out through the kitchen, not wanting to disturb them. It was a lot for Ellie to take in. Funny thing was, he wanted to comfort her, too. He wanted to make everything right. But there wasn't any way that could happen. His company was taking over her life. And if the Flanagans remained in their house Ellie would see it everyday… For awhile he would be here, too, supervising things. He would see her…see her anger…her disdain for what he'd done to her family.

Before he reached the back door, Hugh heard his name called, and he turned to find Ellie coming through the doorway.

"Ellie, I want to tell you I'm sorry—"

"I don't want to hear it, McCutcheon." She glared at him. "What I want you to do is listen to what I have to say."

He nodded.

"You might have gotten my grandfather to agree to your way of thinking, but not me. I'm not giving up…yet." She took a step closer, revealing fire and determination in her green eyes. "I told you there's a hundred years of Flanagan history here. This isn't the first time we've had trouble…and it probably won't be the last."

"I know that, Ellie, and I want to help. I truly do. But my father is serious about this deal."

"Then go back and tell him I'm not giving away this land."

Suddenly there was a loud crash from the dining room.

"Papa," Ellie cried as she shot off.

Hugh was right behind her.

Once in the room, they found Cullan collapsed on the floor.

"Oh, Papa."

They both rushed to his side.

"Sorry, Ellie..." Cullan said, pain etched on his face.

"Don't try to talk," Hugh said as he pulled out his cellphone and called an ambulance, praying that nothing else bad would happen to this family.

Two hours later, Ellie paced the hospital emergency room. She glanced across the seating area to find Hugh leaning against the wall.

She owed him a lot. He'd been right there with her grandfather until the paramedics arrived at the house. He'd followed the ambulance in so she wouldn't be alone.

His concerned gaze caught hers and he walked across the room to her. "You should sit down."

She shook her head and bit her lip to keep from crying. "I can't. If something happens to Papa..."

"Shh." He reached for her and pulled her into a comforting embrace. "He's going to be okay, Ellie. He was awake and alert when they brought him here. And, remember, he wants to hang around to see a couple of great-grandkids."

Ellie felt a tear fall...then another. She wasn't anywhere close to giving him that wish. "I'm a rotten granddaughter. All I think about is having a winery. I never realized how much Papa must have been going through. I'm his only family...and I know he'd love babies to spoil. He would never hurt me unless he had no choice."

Hugh placed his hand across her shoulders and walked her to a private corner to continue their conversation. "Of course you want a winery. That doesn't mean you can't have a family to go with it."

She kept her head lowered. She didn't want him to see her tears. "It does when you can't find time in your life for anything else."

"I know the feeling," he answered with a sigh. "I work too many hours and travel too much."

She finally raised her head. "Do you ever meet anyone

on those travels?" Good Lord, she had no business asking him that.

Hugh wanted to wipe away her tears. "No..." he told her, but added, "Not until I met you."

Those rich green eyes widened, but before she could speak a nurse called her name. She jumped up and hurried across the room. Hugh followed her.

"The doctor will see you now."

Hugh stood still as she started to go, but she turned back. "Will you go with me?"

His heart leaped in his chest. "Of course."

They walked down the hall and met the doctor. "Hello, Ms Flanagan, I'm Dr. Perkins."

She shook his hand. "Nice to meet you, Doctor. This is Hugh McCutcheon...a friend."

He nodded a greeting, then turned to business. "Your grandfather was lucky tonight. With his heart history—"

"What heart history?" Ellie asked. "You mean he's had trouble before?"

"Yes. At his last check-up we talked about him having an angioplasty procedure done. That was three months ago."

"Three months..." she repeated. "He never said anything to me." She seemed to come out of her trance and asked, "Can you still do the Angioplasty?"

"Not without Cullan's permission. See if you can talk some sense into him."

"Consider it done. How soon can you do this procedure?"

"Right away. I don't want him to leave here, so I can schedule it for tomorrow."

"Okay. May I see him?"

He nodded. "I've sedated him, but he'll know you're here."

The nurse took her to a room down the hall. Her grandfather was in a hospital gown and tucked into bed. The machine monitoring his heart was beeping in a steady rhythm. She went to his side and Hugh made his way to the side of the room.

"Papa… It's me—Ellie."

No response.

She leaned over and kissed his cheek. When she pulled back a little, his eyes opened. He looked pale and tired, but he smiled at her.

"My Ellie. I love you, lass." He raised his hand and she grabbed hold.

"I love you, too, Papa. Everything is going to be okay. But the doctor said you need a procedure to help your heart."

"I wanted to wait until later…after the harvest. And I didn't want you to worry about anything more…"

Tears filled her eyes. She couldn't lose him. "Don't you know nothing is more important than you are? Please…Papa, no more arguing. You need this procedure."

"Okay, lass." He swallowed. "Hugh…?" His faint voice called out.

Hugh walked to the man's side. "What is it, Cullan?"

"Will you watch out for Ellie?"

Hugh nodded. "Consider it done."

An hour later, Hugh drove Ellie back to the house. Soft music on the radio was the only sound. Hugh glanced across the car to see Ellie staring out the window into the night.

"He's going to be okay. This procedure is done all the time." He turned the car off the main highway onto the road leading to Emerald Vale.

"I know. I just wish I could have known sooner. So many times I argued with him about a winery. I didn't know how much anxiety he was having about paying back the loan."

"It's not your fault, Ellie. It was his choice not to tell you. He didn't want you to worry."

"So he was destroying his own health to pacify me and my dreams."

"That's because he loves you. And that alone means more to him than any business deal."

Hugh couldn't understand that kind of love. His father

wouldn't lift a hand to help him with anything. Mac didn't have any idea what his son dreamed of. He had to face it, the man wasn't capable of loving him.

Ellie straightened as they pulled up to the house. "Well, Papa doesn't have to worry alone any more. And I'm still not about to let you railroad us into selling." She climbed out of the car.

Hugh got out, too, and caught up to her. "Do you always have to think of me as the enemy?"

"I have to protect myself and my family, Hugh." She pushed open the door, but he reached for her hand.

"I'm not my father," he told her. "I care about what happens here."

She shook her head. "How can I trust you when you go in and destroy companies?"

"I don't destroy companies," he argued. "I go in and try to save them, make them productive again."

"We don't *need* to be any more productive." She glared. "We only need to be left alone."

That hurt. "Fine." Hugh held up his hands. "I'll leave you alone."

Hugh turned and went down the steps, made his way though the yard, along the lighted pathway and into the cottage. He slammed the door shut and began to pace. He wasn't about to sit and relax.

He hadn't done anything wrong. None of this was his fault. He was only the messenger for his father. Usually harsh words didn't hurt him—business was business… But those other words hadn't come from Ellie Flanagan.

An hour later, Ellie knew she owed Hugh an apology. It was late, but she couldn't let it go until morning. She walked up to the cottage, and had started to knock when the door opened and Hugh appeared.

"Is something wrong with Cullan?"

"No. I called the hospital; he's fine."

He gave her the once-over. "Then what is it, Ellie? Did you forget to accuse me of something else?" He leaned against the doorjamb, folding his arms across his chest, looking very unapproachable. "Or did you just want to call me another name?"

"This was a mistake. I'm sorry I bothered you."

She'd turned to leave when her grabbed her arm and pulled her around. "No, I'm the one who's sorry. I know you're under a lot of stress with Cullan."

He didn't release her, and she felt his warmth against her skin. "Without your help…" She couldn't think of any words as she looked up into his eyes. "I don't know what would have happened."

Hugh couldn't let Ellie go. She looked so lost. "I'm glad I was there." Her chin trembled. "Oh, babe, don't…" He pulled her into his arms.

"I can't lose him, Hugh. He's all I have in the world," she sobbed against his shirt.

He held on to her. "I don't want you to be alone, Ellie." He brushed a kiss against her soft hair, inhaling her lemony scent. "I'm here for you."

She pulled back and stared up at him with those wide cat eyes. With his heart pounding, he lowered his head and brushed his lips over hers. She gasped, and he came back again. Another soft touch, brushing her lips. Another nibble…then he drew back.

"Hugh…"

His gaze roamed her face. "You are so beautiful, you take my breath away."

With a shaky smile, she reached up and touched his face. "You're not so bad yourself."

Hugh grinned, then lowered his head again, and this time it wasn't playful. He wanted her to know how she affected him. His mouth slanted over hers in a hungry kiss. He pulled her close against his body, letting her feel all the hard lines while he enjoyed her softness.

He ran his tongue over the seam of her lips until she parted them to allow him in. He groaned as his tongue danced with hers, tasting her sweetness.

Finally he pulled away, and they were both breathless. "Whoa, you pack quite a wallop," he told her as he continued to give her teasing kisses. "And you're tempting me to my limit."

Ellie reached up and placed her mouth against his in another searing kiss. Her hands were at work, parting his shirt.

When her fingertips caressed his skin, he groaned again. Even though he knew this was disastrous, he couldn't stop wanting her. Without breaking the kiss, he swung her up into his arms, kicked the door shut and carried her to the bed in the dimly lit room. He laid her down on the mattress and stretched out beside her.

Okay, this was what he called heaven. He grew serious. "I've wanted you since the moment I first saw you."

Ellie didn't smile as she touched his jaw. "I don't want to be alone, Hugh. I want to stay with you tonight."

"I'm here for you, Ellie." He leaned down and kissed her, moving his hand under her blouse, touching her skin, her breasts. She murmured his name in breathless want as he caressed her.

"Hugh… Please…?" she asked. "Make me forget everything."

Forget. He froze. He couldn't forget his job. Even he couldn't go so low as to seduce Ellie, then go back to business in the morning. Besides, when he made love to Ellie, he wanted her to remember everything that happened between them.

He placed one last kiss on her lips, then pulled back. "Ellie, we can't do this. Not tonight, anyway."

She blinked at him, and desire turned to hurt in her eyes. "Fine. If you don't want me…" She sat up, but Hugh reached for her and pulled her close.

"Wanting is definitely not the problem," he growled. "I want you very much. But you're not ready for this, Ellie. I would just be a distraction for you…and you'd regret what happened between us by morning. I don't want to be just a convenient guy." He pulled her closer. "I want to be here for you…to share your pain, your fears…but when we make love…it has to be because you want me, not because you're hurting."

She buried her face against his chest. "You're right."

He tipped her head up so she'd look at him. "Hey, I'm flattered that you came to me."

"I should go…" She started to sit up, but Hugh couldn't let her go and pulled her back to him. "I don't want you to leave, and I don't think you want to either. Can I just hold you?"

"Maybe…for a little while," she whispered. "I can't seem to sleep, anyway," she said as she went back into his arms.

With Ellie's head resting against his chest, her body snuggled close to his, Hugh fought the feelings she aroused in him. He knew better than to let someone get this close. Besides, it would never work out. He had a job to do. That always came first. It was the safe route for him. He'd watched his own parents' marriage disintegrate, and vowed that he never wanted to chance any commitment.

Not until he'd met Ellie Flanagan. She made him feel things…things he'd never felt before…never allowed himself to feel.

He felt Ellie's body relax and her breathing slow. She was asleep.

He smiled. Yeah, maybe he was a lovesick fool.

CHAPTER SIX

THE first thing Ellie noticed as she began to wake up was the feeling of strong arms wrapped around her. She snuggled deeper, unwilling to leave the protective place. Then a bright glare caused her to blink. Sunlight… Morning… She was in Hugh's bed. Suddenly last night flashed into her head.

She sat up with a jerk. *Papa.*

Hugh groaned and woke up. "Hey, good morning."

She turned around to find his hair mussed, his shirt open, revealing a muscular chest. Something unexpected stirred in her.

"Morning," she said as she scooted off the bed, looking for her sandals. "I need to go to the house and call the hospital… then get to work."

Hugh got up and came around the other side to meet her. "Slow down. Take time for breakfast."

She glanced at the clock. "I can't. I'm usually out in the vineyard by now. I need to talk to the orchard manager, Ben. He wasn't around last night, and they're harvesting the Bartlett pears today."

She slipped on her shoes and headed for the door.

He followed her. "I can help."

She frowned, watching the man who'd been there for her last night. Could she trust him? She had no choice. "Fine. Meet me in the orchard and wear old clothes." She started to leave again, but he grabbed her and pulled her into his arms.

Hugh's mouth came down on hers and immediately turned on the heat between them. When he released her she was slightly dizzy.

He grinned. "I needed a little spark to get me going. Give me ten minutes so I can shower, and I'll catch up to you." He winked. "Unless you want to join me?"

He was enjoying her discomfort too much. Ellie shook her head. "No, I'm fine. See you later." She managed to get out the door. What was wrong with her? She didn't act on impulse—not over a man anyway. And she'd be crazy if she allowed this man to get to her.

She made her way down the back path to the kitchen door, where she saw Ben standing on the stoop.

"Ellie? I can't find Cullan."

She smiled at the fifty-something man who'd worked for the Flanagans for over twenty years. "It's okay, Ben. Papa isn't here. We had to take him to the hospital last night."

"What happened? Was it his heart?"

Ellie paused. Had Ben known about his condition? "Yes, it's his heart, and he was lucky. But he needs to have a procedure done today, so he'll be in the hospital for a few days. If you'll give me a few minutes, I can help with the crew. You know Papa. He'll want a report when I visit him tonight."

The orchard manager smiled as he placed his straw hat on his head. "Then we better get it done."

Ellie went into the house, and rushed upstairs into the room she'd had since she was a teenager. The soft butter walls and the blue accent colors on the bed were welcoming. Grabbing clean clothes, she ran into the bathroom, knowing all that she'd been used to all of her life might be changing very soon.

Twenty minutes later Ellie made her way to the orchard—to find Hugh there. He was picking alongside the other day workers. Her first feeling was that he was invading her domain, and she wanted to chase him off. But another side of her knew she needed all the help she could get, and that if Papa were here he'd put Hugh to work. Silently, she took a basket and walked up to the trees where the branches had been trained to grow across a trellis, much like her grapes.

The fairly new system had helped to increase the trees' density…and fruit. She blinked back the threatening tears, hoping Papa would soon be able to return to what he loved so much.

Hugh appeared next to her. "Did you get some breakfast?"

He'd showered, too, but hadn't shaved. He looked even sexier with his dark-shadowed face. "Just coffee." She continued to twist a pear stem, then placed the fruit carefully in the box. "How about you?"

"I grabbed some coffee and a bagel off the breakfast tray."

She watched him do his task. He gently picked the fruit. She recalled that touch, knew what it could do to her. She shook it away.

"You know, Hugh, you're a guest here. You don't need to do this."

"Even a cold-blooded tycoon like myself wants to help out occasionally. You're just lucky I'm so willing." He smiled, and her heart skipped a beat. "Does it bother you that I'm here?"

More than he'd ever know. "Of course not. But this is a lot of work."

He frowned. "You act like I've never had to roll up my sleeves and pitch in. I'll have you know that I had a paper route when I was twelve. At fifteen I worked in a hamburger joint, and I waited tables in a restaurant all through college."

Ellie had trouble believing that. "I thought your father… I mean, he has the means to…"

"Pay for everything I ever wanted?" he finished as he carefully picked and placed a still-green fruit into the basket. "Hardly. Mac and my mother divorced when I was ten. Besides him not being around much, he didn't believe in handing things out for nothing. 'Hard work builds character', Mac preaches." Hugh smiled. "So I have a lot of character."

It dawned on her that he'd probably worked in a lot of those factories he'd downsized. "How many factory jobs have you done?"

He gave her a sideways glance. "Plenty. You can't improve anything without testing it yourself. So I've had to work for my lucrative salary."

They carried their full boxes and put them into the special bins on the truck. Grabbing an empty, they returned.

"So, when you downsize a business, is it because it's truly needed, or is it strictly for more money?"

He stopped. "If I have to lay off employees, believe me, I don't do it without studying the pros and cons. Otherwise, a plant might be shut down, and then all the workers would lose their jobs, instead of only twenty or thirty percent."

"Your investors still make a lot of money."

"Of course they do. We're all in this to make money."

She frowned. "Not all. Some of us do it because we love what we do."

"I love what I do. But I also love the money I make at my job."

Ellie eyed him closely. "It can't always be about the money. You need more in your life."

Hugh realized he'd enjoyed the morning. He'd liked even more spending time with Ellie.

By noon, they'd loaded the truck, and Ellie now planned to drive it to the packing house. He was surprised when she asked him to go along.

They made the twenty-mile trip without any problems, but the trip back was a different story. The old truck was suddenly temperamental, and decided to quit running.

Ellie coasted to the side of the highway and parked. "So, do you know anything about engines?"

"I'm pretty good at calling a mechanic," he teased. "Or at least a tow truck."

Thirty minutes later they were at a mechanic's shop, with at least an hour to wait while the truck got a new fuel pump.

"We'll be back in a few hours," Hugh told the mechanic. "If there's a problem, call my cellphone number." He took Ellie's arm. "Let's go have some lunch, I'm starving."

Ellie started to argue, but her stomach growled rudely. They both laughed.

"God, you're beautiful when you smile."

She froze. "I'm a mess."

They walked across the parking lot toward a hamburger place. "Good Lord, woman, if I said it was night, you'd say it was day."

"That's because I'd probably be right."

"Just to warn you, arguing turns me on."

She blinked. "I'm sure that makes things interesting in the boardroom."

He threw his head back and laughed. "Okay, I'll rephrase it." He leaned close and whispered, "I get turned on by *you*."

She honestly didn't have a comeback. Especially with his heated gaze on her.

Once inside, they ordered their food at the counter, then found a table and sat down.

Ellie felt strange, sitting across from this man. What was she thinking? She had slept in the same bed with him. He'd kissed her, touched her…and had her wanting more.

"What's the matter, Ellie? Having second thoughts?"

"Second thoughts?"

"About letting the enemy get close to you last night?"

She glanced away, hating the fact that he could read her. "Nothing happened."

"Ah, but we wanted it to, and that's your problem." He leaned forward and whispered, "You wanted me as much as I wanted you."

"Maybe we should talk about something else."

"Look, you had a rough time last night with your grandfather. And I'm just glad I could help you today." He arched an eyebrow. "But that doesn't change the fact that there's an attraction between us."

She grew serious. "Well, I'm not going to get involved with a man who plans to take the Flanagan land."

He didn't answer, but instead went up to retrieve their food order. He set the tray on the table and she took her hamburger.

"I want you to know, Ellie, with Cullan in the hospital I'm going to back off until he's recovered from the procedure."

"What did Mac say about that?"

"To be honest, I haven't talked with my father in a while. This is strictly my decision."

"Papa...Papa..." Ellie said as she stood next to his hospital bed. "It's over, and the doctor said you did great." She had trouble keeping the tears out of her voice.

Finally Cullan opened his eyes. "Then why are you so sad, lass?"

She forced a smile. "Because you're leaving me with all the work."

"Then I better get out of here."

"Tomorrow is soon enough," she told him. "You still need to take it easy, even when you get home."

"I know...but the picking."

"Ben's there," Ellie insisted. "Hugh has helped me, too."

Papa gave her a half-smile. "That doesn't surprise me. He's a good man."

Ellie had to agree. "Ben had him picking pears this morning. He even went with me to the packing house. The old truck broke down on the way back. The fuel pump. It's all fixed, so don't go worrying."

"Told you he's a good man." He closed his eyes a moment. "Now, give me a kiss goodbye, then go home and get some rest, lass."

Ellie did as she was told, then walked out into the hall.

But maybe he could make her forget for a little while.

He took her by the arm and directed her to the elevator. The bell chimed and the door opened. They stepped inside the elevator and the doors closed, leaving them alone. "Let's go get an early dinner."

She blinked at him. "You want to go out?"

"It wouldn't hurt to get away from everything for a few hours."

"Hugh, I don't think it's wise."

He stared at her, not ready to give her up yet. "You slept in my bed last night and you think us sharing a meal isn't wise?" He hesitated. "I'm only talking about a few hours."

"That's what I mean," she began. "I stepped over the line last night with you when I went to your cottage. It's dangerous for us to continue this—"

"This attraction between us," he finished. "Yes, Ellie, I'm definitely attracted to you."

The bell chimed again and the doors opened. They walked off down the corridor. "I enjoy spending time with you. Is that so wrong? Besides, any discussion of the sale is off-limits."

Ellie knew someone was still going to get hurt. And it was probably going to be her.

"And if this sale goes through, I'm going to be around the place."

She didn't like that he was so confident. "It's not final, yet. You never know what might happen." She had a couple of ideas. They were long shots, but she wasn't giving up so easily.

They stepped outside into the cool evening. "Could we call a truce for tonight?"

She had to smile. "I thought you liked heated discussions."

"Come have dinner with me and I'll give you a list of all the other things that get me heated up."

Ellie couldn't remember the last time she'd gone out to dinner with a man other than her grandfather. It was embarrassing, but she hadn't had the time, or met any interesting men, to accept a date.

Hugh surprised her when he drove her to a place called

Porters, a historical train depot that had been converted into a restaurant. It was casual enough for families, but nice enough to take a date. The hostess led them across the dimly lit room to a secluded booth. The bench seats were high-backed, with red curtains tied back to add to their privacy.

"The food here is excellent," Ellie told him.

"So you like the place?"

"I love it here. Although they don't serve our label."

"Well, we should leave, then." He started to get up.

She smiled and placed her hand on his arm. "It's okay, I think I'll manage. Besides, their rosemary roasted prime rib makes up for it."

"So that's your recommendation?"

She nodded. "I've had several dishes here. They're all good."

The waitress came by for their order. Hugh ordered the prime rib for both of them. He let her pick the wine, a Cabernet Sauvignon '03 Del Rio from a local winery.

When the waiter brought the bottle, he opened it, poured red wine into a glass, then gave it to Hugh.

He picked up the goblet and sniffed the bouquet. "I'm following Jillian's instructions." He swirled it, then finally took a drink. He raised an eyebrow. "It's very good. Not as good as the Irish Rogue, but enjoyable."

The waiter smiled and filled a glass for Ellie, leaving the bottle.

She leaned forward. "Have we created a monster?"

"No, but I do want to pick your brain about wine. I am truly out of my element here. This project was supposed to go to someone else—Matt Hudson. He's studied the wine business."

"And you're into manufacturing plants?"

"I'm more into production efficiency."

She played with the stem of her glass. "So if I had a winery it would be easier for you?"

He hesitated. "I think so. I'm good at things like crunching numbers, the depreciation of equipment, efficient use of personnel. Yes, that's my area of expertise."

"So if I ever need someone like that, I'll know who to call."

Hugh wanted to change the direction of the conversation. He reached for her hand. "You don't need a reason to call me, Ellie."

She didn't pull away. "You're a busy man, Hugh McCutcheon. You travel all over the country."

He laced his fingers with hers, feeling her warmth. It was warming him. "I plan to change that. Hopefully, I'll be in San Francisco permanently. Not so far from Medford, Oregon." His gaze met her incredible green eyes, causing feelings he'd never before had for any woman. "You could visit me, too." He was acting crazy, mixing business with...pleasure.

She smiled. "I've visited your city. It was while I was in college."

"I hope you'll want to come back, then. I'd like to take you to The Wharf for some great seafood." There were so many places he wanted to take her.

He didn't wait for an answer as he refilled their glasses, not wanting reality to intrude into this magical evening. Soon their food arrived, and the easy conversation continued all the way though dessert—classic crème brulée—and coffee.

When they left the restaurant, Hugh took her hand and walked her through the parking lot to his car. When they got to the passenger side, he didn't open the door right away.

Hugh gazed into her eyes. "I'm sorry, but I can't wait any longer." He bent his head and captured her mouth. The kiss was controlled, but just barely. It didn't change his need, or the desire he felt for her, but they were in a public place.

He finally tore his mouth away. "Oh, Ellie, you're driving me crazy," he groaned, as he nibbled his way down her neck, then pulled back. "I think I better get you back to the hospital."

Then, with another leisurely kiss, he finally pulled away and opened the door. She climbed in.

Hugh found he was a little shaky as he walked around the car. He got into the driver's seat and started the engine before he succumbed to temptation again. He blew out a breath. Trouble was, even if Ellie Flanagan did come with a warning label, he still wanted her.

And that made for an impossible situation.

About twenty minutes later, Ellie walked into her grandfather's room, wanting to check before heading home. "I don't want you to worry about anything but getting better," she whispered, and placed a kiss against his forehead.

"The same goes for you, Ellie," he murmured as he opened his eyes. "Things will work out."

She knew that was true. Now that she had finally discovered what was most important. "Go back to sleep and I'll see you tomorrow."

"I need to see Hugh first."

"Papa, this isn't the time to talk business."

"Stop worrying, lass." He waved his hand "Now, give me another kiss, then go and send him in."

Ellie did as she was told, then walked into the hall. "Papa wants to talk with you," she told Hugh.

With a nod, Hugh pushed himself off the wall and went in. He couldn't figure out what Cullan could have to say to him.

Lying flat against the white sheet, Cullan Flanagan looked older, and his skin was pale.

Hugh touched his hand. "Cullan..." he whispered.

Ellie's grandfather opened his clear blue eyes. "Hugh..." He raised a limp hand. "I need a favor..."

Hugh leaned closer. "What is it?"

"Ellie... She acts tough...but if something happens to me... she's all alone." He swallowed. "And because of me she's losing something important to her. You've got to help find a way for her to keep at least part of the vineyard. Maybe the original vines her daddy planted..."

Hugh didn't want to hear this kind of talk. "Whoa, Cullan,

you're not to worry about any of that now. I promise I won't discuss anything about the sale until you're well." He squeezed his hand. "We'll discuss this then. And I'll make sure Ellie is fine."

A faint smile appeared across Cullan's face. "I knew I could depend on you. You're a good man." He closed his eyes and was asleep.

A good man? He didn't feel like a good man at all. What kind of man would take advantage of this situation…of a woman? He turned to see an anxious Ellie in the hall. His heart pounded. He knew he wanted to take her in his arms and tell her everything was going to be all right. He couldn't. He couldn't offer her one damn thing—except maybe some honesty.

CHAPTER SEVEN

ON THE drive home, the car was filled with music, but not much conversation. Ellie was almost afraid to ask what her grandfather had said, but she knew that something had changed the moment Hugh walked out of the hospital room.

Hugh parked in front of the house and got out, started to walk her toward the porch. She stopped him.

"Please, I don't want to go in just yet," she said. "I need to walk."

He nodded, and she led him toward the rose garden. Soft exterior lights lit their way along the path and through the gate. Ellie immediately caught a whiff of the familiar rose fragrance. She felt her grandmother's presence.

"I like to come here when I can't sleep or I need to think about things..." She looked up at him. "Thank you for taking me to dinner tonight."

Hugh didn't want her gratitude. "It wasn't a big deal," he lied. Every minute he spent with Ellie Flanagan was a big deal...but that was about to come to an end.

"I guess that's the difference between us. You're probably used to going out, sharing wine and a few casual kisses... I'm not."

"There is nothing casual about you, Ellie," he insisted. "And I don't make a habit of taking out potential clients and seducing them."

She took a step closer and slipped her arms around his neck. "Are you trying to seduce me, Hugh McCutcheon?"

He closed his eyes, feeling her soft feminine body pressed against his.

"I think you're the one doing the seducing," he told her, then lost any resolve as he lowered his head and captured her mouth. Wrapping his arms around her back, he dragged her even closer against him. He wanted a permanent imprint of her… He wanted to remember the taste of her on his lips…

But he couldn't allow it to happen… He broke off the kiss. "We should stop."

"Why?" she breathed.

"I don't want to take advantage, Ellie. I know you're worried about Cullan…"

Ellie paused and studied his face, then moved back. "Does this have anything to do with what my grandfather said to you at the hospital?"

"Not in the way you think," he told her. "But he made me see things differently." He caught the wariness in her mesmerizing eyes. "Look, Ellie. This whole situation with Emerald Vale makes it impossible for anything… between us."

She glanced away, then back at him. "That could change."

He froze. "I don't see how?"

"I've changed my mind about a lot of things since Papa's health scare. I've discovered what's important. My grandfather is my main concern now. I know the pressure of this loan has to be making his life miserable." She sighed. "I'm selfish enough to want him to hang around for another dozen or so years. I'm willing to give up the land."

Hugh stared at her.

Hugh was caught off guard by Ellie's decision. He knew how much she'd looked forward to building a winery. "What about your dream? You're a winemaker."

She shook her head, but she couldn't hide her emotions. "If I have Papa and some of the old Flanagan land, I'll be happy."

They both knew it was a lie, but Hugh wasn't going to argue the point now. "Let's hold off on this decision until your grandfather is out of the hospital."

"I'm not going to change my mind, Hugh. I mean it. I won't fight you about selling." Her voice lowered. "I don't want this to come between us."

"Oh, Ellie…" He pulled her back into a tight embrace, kissed her long and hard, then released her. "God, you're tearing me apart."

"Is that a good thing?" she asked teasingly.

He couldn't go on like this. This was a no-win situation, and he was caught in the middle. "No. Don't you see that business would always come between us?"

"Then walk away from it," she challenged. "The business, I mean…"

"And if I do the bank or someone else will come in here, and you and Cullan will lose everything anyway."

Her mouth was still swollen from his kisses. "So you're saying business comes first?"

"In this instance, yes." He *couldn't* get involved with her, he chanted over and over. His father was ruthless enough to destroy them all.

In the dim light, he watched her blink back tears as her chin came up. "I guess there's nothing more to say."

"I wish it could be different…"

"Please, don't say any more." She stared at him. "Goodbye, Hugh."

With no choice, he had to let her go. He was about to take away her dream…and he knew someday she would come to hate him.

When Ellie got up the next morning Hugh McCutcheon was still on her mind…along with his distracting kisses and his hurtful rejection.

She'd been a fool. Hugh McCutcheon was only after one

thing, and it wasn't her. It was the Flanagan property. Now she'd told him she was willing to sell the land, he was moving on.

Well, so was Ellie. She decided she wasn't giving up so easily. She dressed in a print skirt, a royal blue sweater and comfortable pair of sandals, and headed to her car. Ben could handle the harvesting today while she went and brought Papa home. But first she had to talk to a man about getting a loan. She wasn't going to give up everything without finding some other options…

She was determined to fight to keep her heritage.

In the orchard, Hugh emptied another basket of pears into the bin, hoping work would distract him. It didn't. He'd let Ellie get to him. He'd realized that last night when he'd kissed her… and kissed her again. The only choice he had was to cool things off. He had to keep his distance.

Ellie tempted him like no other woman, but he had to find a way to keep focused on his job, because in the end someone would get hurt.

Suddenly his phone rang. He walked away from the other workers and checked the ID to see his father's name. Why not? It had been days. But he couldn't talk to the man now, and let the call go to voicemail.

He cursed. Not at his father, but at the situation. He didn't want Cullan to lose his orchard, nor did he want Ellie to lose the vineyard. It wasn't right. Damn, he hated this. Before he'd come here his job had always been just a building, a business that an owner could walk away from.

How did you walk away from your life?

That evening, Ellie helped her grandfather out to the porch. "Just sit there and rest," she instructed him as she brought him a glass of lemonade. He could watch the sunset over the orchard.

"That's all I've done since I've gotten home."

"And if you want to attend the Stewarts' anniversary party this coming weekend, that's all you're doing—until the doctor says differently."

"Could you at least tell me if Ben finished up today?" he asked.

"I haven't talked to him personally, but he'll be up in a little while to tell you himself." She knew Papa wouldn't rest until he knew everything about the harvest. Since he'd been a boy, the orchard had been his way of life. He'd bragged that he'd never gotten a paycheck for a job.

This was Cullan Flanagan's life. She was going to do everything possible for him to keep it all.

The next evening, Hugh stood on the patio drinking a glass of wine. Ellie was working in the vineyard. Although he was a distance away, he could see the enthusiasm in her movements… her walk. The way she talked and laughed with the workers. No doubt she knew them all by their names… He smiled. She had told him they were all family. Loneliness nearly consumed him as he thought about how he'd walked away from her. It was for the best, he told himself. And he knew he had to keep away. He couldn't get involved with her, then turn around and try to put together a business deal for Mac. Maybe it would help if he honestly felt his father was turning this transaction into something good.

Had Mac always been such a heartless businessman? His father was a millionaire several times over. He didn't have to go after a business—especially one that just needed a little help. Did Mac have to take *everything* from them?

There had to be another way. The Flanagans didn't want to be millionaires, just to keep their family's land. Hugh found he was envious of what Ellie had: her close relationship with Cullan, and her family's history right here in the Valley.

Something he would never have. Not because he couldn't. He just wouldn't allow himself to take a chance at love and a try for a family. The chance his parents had failed at. But that didn't mean he hadn't dreamed about having it all with someone like Ellie.

"I see she hasn't lost her appeal for you."

Hugh turned to see Cullan standing on the path. He was embarrassed that he'd been caught…once again. "It's hard not to stare. She's a beautiful woman."

"Aye, and so much more, too. She has a true heart." Cullan looked back at him. "I thought you could see that, too."

Hugh knew a lot about Ellie Flanagan, but he'd always be hungry for more. "I do. But with everything going on I can't get involved with Ellie."

Cullan continued his journey up the path and stood on the patio beside Hugh. "So you are going to go because of the business between us?"

"That's a valid enough reason," he told him. "I've already come between you two. Ellie loves you, Cullan, and I can't be the cause of her unhappiness."

Cullan studied him for a moment. "Did I misjudge you, lad? I thought you were smart enough to figure out what you truly want and what Ellie needs."

Hugh doubted Cullan was talking about the regional director's job at McCutcheon.

"You need to figure out what is truly important in life." Cullan turned back to the woman in the vineyard. "It might be right in front of you."

Oh, yes, he wanted Ellie Flanagan. "I know what I want, sir. I just can't have it."

"So you give up so easily on love? Maybe you should just work harder on a solution."

That following Saturday, Ellie was still trying to add the final touches to the scheduled event. She walked around the garden, checking each decorated table. White linen with red roses as the centerpieces. Usually she loved doing weddings and parties in the garden, but it had been an overwhelming week.

Still, Ellie needed to make the Stewarts' fiftieth wedding

anniversary party something special. It had been scheduled for nearly a year.

Of course she hadn't foreseen the fact that her grandfather would have heart trouble, or that the property was going to be up for sale.

Speaking of the vulture, where *was* Hugh McCutcheon? Not that she was looking, she reminded herself. But over the last few days she'd barely seen the man. Not since their so-called date. The last time he'd kissed her… The last time she'd dared to hope that he was going to be on their side. She'd been crazy enough to believe that something had happened between them. That Hugh could possibly be the man she'd dreamed about…the man she might fall in love with. But he had made his choice, and that told her he wasn't the man she'd thought he was.

The soft music from the quartet brought her back from her musings. She stood back to check that everything was coming together, and noticed the arrival of some guests. Thanks to Jillian, they were being escorted into the tasting room for now.

She brushed off her dress. It was sleeveless, with a scooped neck and a bias-cut tea-length skirt of teal and pale yellow. Her ivory sandals were high-heeled, with thin straps that fastened around her ankles. She wore her hair up and her grandmother's pearls around her neck.

She looked up, and a man caught her eye as he walked through the gate. Hugh. He looked devastatingly handsome, dressed in a dark suit and a snowy-white shirt with a conservative burgundy tie.

She wasn't happy that he could still set her pulse to racing, making her entire body aware of him. What was he doing here? Then her grandfather walked in and stood next to him. She smiled, seeing how distinguished he looked in his navy suit. Her gaze moved back to Hugh, then to her grandfather. Both men were handsome, had stubborn streaks, and both had plenty of charm. She suddenly realized she loved them both.

* * *

"Now, lad, don't do anything to rile her," Cullan warned him, then smiled at Ellie.

Hugh wasn't convinced coming tonight was a good idea. "She isn't going to want me here."

"Then I guess you better change her mind."

He glanced across the garden to see Ellie in a soft floral dress that showed off her shapely body. Although he liked her hair down, wearing it up exposed her lovely neck.

She approached them. "Papa, you look so handsome." She worked to straighten his tie. "Remember, just don't overdo it."

"I feel fine, and I've already promised Amanda Stewart a dance." He winked. "I want one with you, too."

"A slow one." She turned to Hugh. "Hugh, are you dressed up for some reason?"

"I hear there's a party tonight. I've been invited by Cullan."

He watched her expression. She wasn't happy.

"I introduced him to Jim and Amanda," her grandfather told her. "They insisted he come to the party. So put him at our table." Papa waved at someone. "Excuse me, I see some friends." He strolled off, leaving Hugh with Ellie.

"Sorry to mess up your table arrangements…" he began. "I'll sit anywhere you put me."

She raised her chin a notch. "I can't understand why you want to attend anyway."

He shrugged, but he was far from indifferent. "I guess I'm discovering what's important—friends and family celebrating a milestone."

"I wasn't even sure you were still here," she told him.

"I had some business to tie up."

She sighed. "Isn't it always about business with you?"

"I guess it has been…in the past. But can't a guy change?"

"You can do what you please, Hugh. I have no hold on you."

"You might be surprised." He smiled.

"I'm not sure I know what you mean."

He took a step closer and caught a whiff of her perfume. "How about we just enjoy the evening and see where it leads?"

He saw her face flush. She was interested. "I have to work."

"I can help. Show me what you need done."

When those big green eyes locked with his, it nearly brought him to his knees. His chest tightened with the sudden rush of feelings he'd never experienced before.

She didn't seem to be able to break the contact either.

"Ellie…"

She shook her head. "Okay…you can help. Go find Father Reyes. He's in the tasting room, but we should have him here, and ready to begin with the renewing of the Stewarts' wedding vows."

Hugh smiled. "So I look for a guy with a white collar and bring him to the garden? I think I can handle that." He started to walk away, then turned back to her. "Ellie, I said some things last week that I didn't think through."

She blinked. "You don't owe me any explanation."

Yes, he did. And he would tell her everything very soon. He nodded. "Will you save me a dance?"

"Hugh…I'm working. Besides, there'll be plenty of women here to dance with."

"But they're not you. I want you, Ellie."

The party was going perfectly, Ellie thought as she watched the older couple on the dance floor. They'd renewed their vows, and there hadn't been a dry eye in the place. The large wedding cake had been cut by the bride and groom, and they'd playfully fed each other the sweet confection. And many, many kisses had been shared between them.

And now the dancing had started, with the big band sound that Jim and Amanda Stewart had fallen in love to. They looked so happy as they moved smoothly around the floor. She knew that over their fifty years there had been problems and fights, but to see how they looked at each other today was so heartwarming. They had four adult children and eleven grandchildren who were cheering them on.

Someday would she be dancing with her husband? Ellie wondered. Would she have children? She'd been so busy working that the years were quickly passing by, and she was getting pretty close to thirty.

"They look happy."

Ellie turned around to see Hugh. "They are. I've known the Stewarts since I was a child. Jim has always treated his wife as if they were newlyweds."

"That's rare—especially with the divorce rate so high."

He was so cynical. "It was a different generation. They survived the Depression and the Second World War."

"Are you saying our generation gives up too easily?"

"Maybe," Ellie conceded. "Seems we've become a disposable society these days. We need to hold on to some of our past."

He paused a moment, knowing she was talking about her situation. "Not all people work hard for what they want." He leaned closer. "When I find something I want, you can bet I'm going to work hard to keep it."

"A wife isn't a possession," she argued. "She needs to be partner…in everything. That might be the reason so many marriages don't survive. A lot of men can't accept that."

"Whoa…" He grinned. "Don't put me in that category. I happen to like strong women, but I'm not so sure marriage is a great union."

She saw a flash of pain in his eyes before he masked it. His parents' divorce had caused scars. "I hope you change your mind. Look around. There are a lot of happily married couples right here."

To her surprise, he did glance around at the couples dancing. And when the music changed to a romantic 1940s ballad, Hugh escorted her to the dance floor and pulled her into his arms. "Maybe it's contagious." His breath was against her ear.

"It's also a slower pace here in the valley." She leaned back and looked up at him. "A simpler life."

His grip tightened as her body fit against his. "Is that the secret, Ellie?"

She looked at him. "No, Hugh. The secret is to love someone so deeply you can't live without them...no matter what happens."

CHAPTER EIGHT

"NOTHING is ever perfect," Ellie told Hugh as they swayed to the music. "But if you find someone you want to share your life with, it can feel perfect."

Hugh didn't want to get into an argument with her. All he wanted was to spend time with her, enjoy this time together. "Having you in my arms feels pretty perfect to me," he whispered, close to her ear. Tightening his hold, he pressed her softness against his body, and heat shot through him.

He wanted to forget everything else but them. That would be an ideal world. To have Ellie close to him always. The admission threw him. But it was true. He did want Ellie more than he'd ever wanted any woman.

"You're a good dancer," she said.

"Thank you," he said. "We fit together pretty well."

Her rich green eyes met his. "Yes, we do."

Her candor surprised him. "Thanks for letting me crash the party."

"I had nothing to do with it. You were invited."

He raised an eyebrow. "That's not exactly true. Cullan told Jim I was your date."

She blinked. "My date? But why? Why did you want to come to the party?"

Hugh took her hand and led her off the dance floor. He stopped at the side of the house, beside the high hedges and away from the crowd. He turned to her as the moonlight reflected off her hair and her pretty face. The sound of music and guests' voices began to fade as he was mesmerized by her.

"Ellie, I wanted to come to the party…to be with you."

"With me… But you were the one who walked away."

He stepped closer. "And I've stayed away because I thought it was the best thing to do. But there was one thing that I didn't figure on."

She swallowed. "What was that?"

"How much I would miss you…miss talking with you… joking with you…even arguing with you."

She lowered her eyes and timidly admitted, "I've missed you too…"

He released a breath. "So tonight… I want to forget everything else and be with you."

"Be we can't…" she said.

He pressed his forehead against hers. "We have this week… we can forget about business." He wanted more time with her, but he'd take what he could get. "Believe me, when I'm around you I'm definitely not thinking about acquisitions." He released a breath. "How can I when all I have on my mind is how badly I want to kiss you?"

Ellie ran her hands up his shirt, over his shoulders, and locked them behind his neck. "Tell me how bad," she teased, and pressed her mouth against his briefly.

"Bad." He dipped his head and attempted to kiss her, but she pulled back.

"Do you think about me all day?"

He nodded. "And all night…" He cupped the back of her head and held her close. "I dream about you…ache for you. All I can think about is holding you in my arms, touching you… making love to you."

"Oh, my…"

Hugh gave her a smile. "Is that all you can say?"

Her wide eyes roamed over his face. "Kiss me, Hugh."

He didn't make her wait. He bent his head and captured her

mouth. His tongue ran over her lips, then delved inside and tasted her sweetness.

"Oh, Ellie. I could get addicted to this…to you." He wanted her, and one night would never be enough. He kissed her again and again, trying to memorize her taste…her touch.

Then their private world was interrupted, when someone called Ellie's name. She looked up to see one of the workers.

"I need to get back to the party." She pulled away, but he stopped her.

"I'll let you go if you promise to come back. I want more time with you, Ellie." He paused. "I think you want the same thing."

She hesitated. "The party will go on for a few more hours."

"Let me help you."

She shook her head. "I'll never get anything done. It probably won't be until about midnight before I can get away."

"I'll be at the cottage…waiting for you." He kissed her again and finally released her. She hurried down the path, and it took every ounce of his will-power to keep from going after her.

Hugh followed the path to the cottage, realizing that, as much as he'd tried, he'd gone and fallen hard for Ellie Flanagan. And that meant if he wanted a future with her…something had to give. He had to make sure Cullan and Ellie didn't lose Emerald Vale.

The only problem was he could lose everything he'd worked for. But that didn't seem to matter to him anymore.

Hugh stopped, noticing a light on the cottage patio. When he got closer, he found a man sitting at the table. It wasn't just any man. It was his father.

"Well, it's about time you got here," Mac said as he stood.

"Hello, Mac." Hugh wasn't going to give in to the man. "It would have been nice if you'd let me know you were coming."

"I wasn't sure myself," Mac told him. "But you've been

dragging your feet, boy. So I thought you needed to be set straight."

Great. At the age of thirty-two, he was getting lectured. "Set straight? I'm not a child. And I don't appreciate you looking over my shoulder while I do my job."

"I'll look when it concerns me," his father warned. "Especially if you aren't doing what you were sent here to do."

Hugh remained silent as he studied Mac. Funny, people always said they looked alike, but he hoped the similarity didn't go any further than appearances. Mac McCutcheon was condescending, rude and arrogant. He treated people with disdain.

"I can't force Cullan Flanagan to sell the land."

"But you can pressure him."

"The man just got out of the hospital," Hugh told him. "I'm not going to do anything to harm his recovery."

"Then maybe you aren't the man for the job."

Hugh tried not to react. Not to protect himself, but he knew Mac wouldn't hesitate to send another vulture to hound Cullan. He had to handle this his way. "Don't worry, Mac. I'll get you results."

Ellie quickened her pace to the cottage. Thanks to Jillian, who'd offered to handle the clean-up for her, she was free to go be with Hugh.

She tried to contain her excitement, but it wasn't possible—not even with all the warning signs that popped up. Nothing could curtail her resolve to be with Hugh tonight.

It would more than likely be their only time together. There was no possible future for them. Once Papa signed the papers the vineyard would be gone, along with her dream...and Hugh.

Ellie reached the patio, realizing that he was the one she didn't want to end things. Did he feel the same? Could they come up with some sort of long-distance relationship? She walked to the door, found it open, and heard voices—men's voices.

Who was with Hugh? She peered inside to see an older man, with thick gray hair. He was trim and well dressed, in a dark suit. Hugh's father. Mac McCutcheon. They were involved in conversation and didn't notice her.

"Don't worry, Mac. I'll get you results."

"Don't drag this out any longer. I've seen Flanagan's granddaughter, and it seems to me you could make her agreeable to this deal."

Hugh nodded. "I said I would handle it."

Ellie suddenly felt sick. But before she could get away, Hugh saw her.

"Ellie… What are you doing here?"

The look on his face would be almost laughable if she wasn't so hurt. "I was invited. But I see you already have a guest."

Mac McCutcheon immediately came to her. "It's a pleasure to meet you, Ellie. My son has told me so much about you."

He extended his hand to her. She refused to take it.

"Stop with the phony charm, Mr. McCutcheon. I'm not falling for it. And if I have any influence with my grandfather, he'll never sell the land to you or your company."

The man didn't even blink. "I'm sorry to hear that. I can guarantee you the McCutcheon Corporation will give you the best deal, and a large amount of money."

She hated this, and had to fight to keep from running away. "It's not always about money, Mr. McCutcheon." She finally looked at Hugh. "But I couldn't get that through to your son… so I'm not going to waste my time with you."

She squared her shoulders. "Emerald Vale is not for sale… to you." She turned and marched out.

She heard Hugh calling her, but she didn't stop. He finally reached her.

"Please, Ellie. You have to listen to me. I had no idea he was coming here."

"Sorry to spoil it." She fought her tears. "Tell me, Hugh, was seduction part of your plan?"

"Please, Ellie. What happened between you and me had nothing to do with business. I told you the truth. Until your grandfather was well, I wouldn't discuss the deal with him."

She crossed her arms to try and stop her trembling, to stop her pain. What a fool she'd been. She had given her heart and love to this man and he'd thrown it back at her. "But there wasn't anything stopping you from softening up the granddaughter."

Hugh felt as if she'd slapped him. He wished for physical pain, because what he felt inside was killing him. "If that's what you truly believe of me then I'm wasting my time."

She didn't speak. "What am I supposed to believe, Hugh? Your father shows up here…and I find you collaborating with him."

The pain grew worse. "I'll be packed and gone by morning. Goodbye, Ellie."

He turned and headed back to the cottage. The only thing worse was Mac being inside.

"So you couldn't get her to listen?" his father asked.

"No, I couldn't get her to listen. But I haven't given up."

"Don't tell me you've fallen for the girl?" Mac began to pace. "That could be good."

"Just stop. This is not about business anymore. I want you to leave."

"I'll leave when I'm good and ready."

Hugh closed his eyes. He was so tired of this. "No, you're not giving orders now. Not here. I'm going to protect Cullan and Ellie from you."

"How dare you talk to me—?"

"It's time someone stood up to you." He moved forward. "All during my childhood I wanted your attention, your love. Later I would have settled for your acceptance. I never got it. Not even in the last eight years I've worked for the company."

"Don't you see I had to be harder on you because you were my son? I couldn't show favoritism."

"You didn't have to worry about that. I've never been your son. Not truly. You only wanted me around because I produce so well. And I was stupid enough to do anything to try to please you." He paused. "It's never going to happen. Because I'm not trying any more. I quit."

"You can't be serious. You're giving up everything you've worked for because of a woman?"

Hugh clenched his fists. "Yes, because of a woman. And because I found a conscience."

Mac looked him over and paused. "It seems you've found your backbone, too. It's about time. You're the kind of man I want as my regional director." He grinned. "The job's yours, son."

Hugh couldn't believe it. For the past year the man had dangled the position under his nose and he'd worked his butt off trying to earn it.

Funny thing was, he didn't want it anymore. "No, I don't want it." He leaned closer. "I don't think I need to tell you what you can do with the regional director's job. Goodbye, Mac."

Ellie hid out in her bedroom, praying that Hugh wouldn't come looking for her. She fought the tears. She wouldn't give Hugh McCutcheon the satisfaction. Not even if her world was crumbling and she could do nothing to stop it.

A soft knock sounded on her door, then her grandfather's voice.

She sat up. "Come in."

He peered in the door and smiled. "What's wrong, lass? Are you sick?"

She shook her head. "I'm just tired. So many things have happened the past few weeks. Your illness and..." Hugh's deception, she added silently.

He sat down on the bed. "You shouldn't have to worry about these things, Ellie. I never meant for this to happen."

"Please, Papa. It's not important. We have our home and the old orchard." She forced a smile. "And we have each other.

We're still a family. You always taught me family is everything. The love and pride of the Flanagans."

They both laughed. "Your grandmother would be so proud of you."

"And I was proud of her."

Papa touched her chin. "I wish she was here now to help you. I'm not very good with matters of the heart."

She blinked, but, seeing the knowing look in Papa's eyes, she couldn't deny anything. "It's okay. There's nothing to worry about. I misjudged Hugh. He'll be leaving soon."

"Can you tell me what happened?"

"After the party…I was to meet him at his cottage." She saw the gleam in her grandfather's eye and she blushed.

"What? You think you kids invented love?" he asked her. "Your grandmother and I sneaked around more than once to find time alone." He sighed, as if remembering that time. "Her father was pretty strict. But I was heading off overseas during the war, so we had to meet when there was opportunity. I told her I loved her the day I got on the train, and that I'd be back for her. She was there waiting for me. Then I went to her father and asked for her hand in marriage."

Ellie had heard the story many times, but she loved hearing Papa tell it. "Not all love stories turn out that happily."

He studied her a moment. "Have you listened to Hugh's explanation?"

"I overheard what Hugh said to his father. He said he'd get *results*."

"Maybe he was talking about the business deal?" Papa told her. "I'm a pretty good judge of character. I believe that Hugh has feelings for you. Everything he's done here shows me that he isn't just out for the almighty dollar. I saw him watching you in the vineyard. He looked heartsick. He even came to me and asked about coming to the party…to be with you."

Ellie wanted to be hopeful, but she knew what she'd heard. "Then why did he say those things to his father?"

"I don't know. But maybe you should ask him. Give him a chance to explain."

Ellie was tired of explanations, excuses. He was going to take her land. There couldn't be any future for them. Not ever.

The doorbell rang, and her grandfather got up. "It's probably Jillian leaving me the key." He leaned over and kissed her. "Get some sleep. We'll deal with this tomorrow."

Ellie rolled on her side and closed her eyes, but it didn't change anything. She couldn't shut off her feelings for the man, probably never would.

Hugh was about to pound on the door when Cullan opened it. "I need to see Ellie."

"I don't think she's ready to talk to you right now."

Cullan stepped aside to let him into the entry. There was a large oriental rug covering hardwood floors. The staircase leading upstairs had a carved railing that swept up gracefully to the second floor. He wished for Ellie to appear, to let him tell her his feelings.

"I need to talk to her…to explain what happened. I had no idea my father would show up."

"Is that the real problem?"

Hugh raked his hand through his hair and cursed. "No, it's not. That the reason I'm pulling out of the deal. And I quit my job. I can't take the vineyard away from Ellie. I know how much she loves it."

Cullan nodded. "I know, but your pulling out isn't going to stop the sale. I still can't meet the balloon payment. And I'm a proud man, Hugh. Flanagans have always paid their debts… and I owe that money."

Cullan took Hugh into the parlor. He suddenly felt as if he'd stepped back fifty years. There was an ornate loveseat and matching chair in front of a marble fireplace. The centerpiece of the room was a grand piano, and on top was a cluster of pictures. Some very old.

Cullan picked one up. "This is my Eleanor."

In the sepia-colored picture Hugh couldn't tell hair or eye color, but there was no doubt that Ellie was the image of her grandmother. "Ellie looks so much like her."

"I know. They're so much alike. Both women loving and giving…and maybe a little stubborn." He replaced the picture and began to point out some other members of the family.

"Through the decades there have been some colorful characters who've worked this land. I just hate that I have to lose it for future generations."

"If you're willing to listen, I've come up with some possible ideas on how to handle the loan payment."

The older man studied him a moment, then grinned. "I knew you'd come through."

Hugh raised a hand. "I haven't, yet. I still have to iron out some things. So don't say anything to Ellie. I don't want to get her hopes up."

"I think the only thing that would get Ellie's hopes up would be if you didn't walk out of her life."

Hugh's chest tightened. Was there still hope for him? Would she forgive him? "Then I'm going to fight for her, Cullan."

The older man slapped him on the back. "I knew you were the right one for my girl."

"Let's pray she feels the same way."

The next week was terrible for Ellie. She had wanted Hugh to leave, and now he was gone. No goodbye, no *I'll see you,* just an empty room…and her aching heart. The only thing she could do was to try and stay busy in the vineyard with the upcoming harvest. This would be her last for Irish Rogue.

Her grandfather seemed healthy…and happy. There were only a few weeks left until the payment was due. She'd expected to have her grandfather make a decision on selling. Since there hadn't been any more offers for the property, she figured he was selling to the McCutcheon Corporation. She hated that. So much so, she wanted to move off the property completely.

She didn't want to be anywhere around Hugh. But she couldn't leave Papa.

She needed to concentrate on looking for a job. Henry Blackford had been asking her for years. Maybe she could go to work for Blackford Winery. Maybe she could do something completely different and get a job in town. There wouldn't be much to do around the old orchard.

Of course she still had a schedule of weddings the following weekend, and several more until the end of the summer. The weddings and parties provided a good income, and they still needed the revenue.

Ellie stood on the hill and looked down at the rows of vines woven around trellises heavy with clusters of grapes. It was going to be a good harvest this year.

Her last. A tear fell.

"Are you okay, lass?" her grandfather asked.

She wiped her eyes. "I should be asking you that. But, yes, I'm okay. I'm just making peace."

Papa drew her close. She loved his strength and the fact he'd always been there for her. He'd never let her down.

"I love you, Ellie." He hugged her tighter. "And it's going to be okay. Please believe me."

She wanted to, but not much could restore her faith.

"Okay, I'll admit I was wrong," Mac said.

Hugh actually stopped clearing out his desk in the San Francisco office, and looked at him. "What?"

"I said I was wrong. You could have handled the Flanagan deal. I never should have showed up in Medford. There—I said it."

"You're only saying that because you lost."

"There's no reason to rub it in my face. I still have three other vineyards."

"But you want the Emerald Vale land."

He shrugged. "I just don't like to lose."

"You can't have everything."

"I know I want you as regional director."

Mac was too late for that. "That's one of the things you can't have. I've resigned."

"Think of the money you're passing up."

"I have a lot of money. And it hasn't made me happy. There's got to be something else out there."

His father studied him. "So you let her get to you?"

"If you mean Ellie Flanagan, oh, yes, she got to me all right. And I'm going to do everything I can to win her back."

Mac shook his head.

"Come on, Dad. Don't you get lonely sometimes? I mean, it can't be all about the thrill of running a business."

He shrugged. "Maybe. But no woman could put up with my work schedule."

Hugh saw a flash of a different man. "Maybe you should seek some counseling; it might help you. All I know is I don't want to end up like you."

"Hey, it's not so bad."

Hugh tossed the last of his files in a box and glanced around one more time, then looked at his father. "That's because you were never the kid who longed to spend time with his father. No, I'm never going to be like you. And if I'm lucky enough to have a family, I'm going to put my wife and kids first. Too bad you didn't, Dad. I might not be leaving now."

CHAPTER NINE

THE following week Hugh drove his rental car along Interstate 5, just outside Medford, Oregon. It was hard to believe it had been a month since he first came here.

Since the first time he'd seen Ellie.

It had taken him a while, but he'd finally realized she was everything he could ever want, and he didn't want to live without her. Now all he had to do was convince her they could make a life together.

He turned off at the exit and drove down the highway until he saw the road leading to Emerald Vale. Soon rows of vines appeared on one side of the road, then the orchard came into view on the other side.

A strange feeling came over him, as he realized this was where he wanted to be. He drove through the gate, passed the house and the general store, then parked and climbed out of the car. He had the papers on the seat beside him—the contracts that could help everyone get what they want.

He closed the door and walked into the empty store. He continued to the tasting room, and saw Jillian working behind the counter.

She smiled. "Well, look what wandered in."

"Hi, Jillian."

"Welcome back, stranger. Are you just stopping by? Or are you hanging around awhile?"

Hugh opened his mouth, but he didn't get a chance to talk. Someone else spoke for him.

"He won't be staying at all."

Hugh turned around to find Ellie. She was dressed in her usual work clothes of jeans, boots and blouse. Her hair was braided, but some curls had pulled free. She looked beautiful.

God, he'd missed her. "Hello, Ellie. It's good to see you again."

"I can't say the same," she announced. "I think it would be best if you leave. This is still Flanagan property."

"I'm here to talk with your grandfather."

She folded her arms over her chest. "I'm not interested in anything you have to say…and I doubt he is either."

Hugh caught the trembling of her hands. He hoped it was an indication that he still had an effect on her. "I seem to recall you saying nearly those same words to me the first time I came here."

She raised her chin. "You should have listened then. It would have been better for all of us."

"As I said before," he began again. "I came to see your grandfather."

"I won't have you causing trouble for him again—"

That hurt. "Give me some credit, Ellie. Since when have I intentionally hurt Cullan? And if you think I don't care about the man, then you haven't been paying attention." He drew a breath. "But I can see I'm wasting my breath." He stormed out of the store.

"Wait," she called. "Hugh, wait."

He was beside the car before he turned around. "What? You remembered some more choice words for me, huh, Ellie?"

She shook her head. "I'm sorry. My grandfather is in the orchard." Then she hurried off.

Hugh wanted to call her back. But not yet. He didn't have it all finalized. He needed to talk to Cullan first.

He grabbed his briefcase off the front seat, and was headed toward the orchard when Cullan appeared.

They met halfway. "Good to see you, Hugh. Let's go to the house and you can tell me what you came up with."

"It's not exactly what we talked about, but I think it might work."

Cullan smiled. "I already like the idea that you tried to help." He paused on the porch step. "I'll never forget that, son."

Hugh nodded, unable to speak.

Once seated at the dining room table, Hugh opened the briefcase and took out the first agreement.

"You have good neighbors and friends, Cullan. And you're well respected here in the community. I talked with—"

"Grandfather…"

They both looked up to see Ellie standing in the doorway. "Does this meeting have anything to do with the loan payment?"

"Yes, it does, lass."

"Then I have a lot at stake here, too. So may I sit in on the meeting?"

"I would never make any decision without you, Ellie. Hugh just has some ideas that might help us."

She turned those sultry green eyes on him. "Hugh, may I stay?"

He couldn't deny her anything. When he nodded, she walked in and sat down across from him at the table.

Hugh didn't want to look at her. He didn't need the distraction. He placed the contract in front of Cullan.

"I talked our idea over with Henry Blackford last week, and after he discussed it with his lawyer he got back to me yesterday. His lawyer drew up this contract."

Ellie frowned. "What did you discuss with Henry?"

Hugh spoke. "I offered Henry an option to buy the vineyard…at the same price as the bank loan."

She gasped. "But the vineyard is worth so much more."

Hugh nodded. "Before you get upset, let me explain."

She sat back in her chair.

"Here's the stipulation," he began, turning his attention to Cullan. "Henry owns the land for the next five years, and takes half the profits of the wine. But after the agreement term ends, he sells the vineyard back to you—and only you."

Ellie couldn't believe it. "Why would Henry want to do that? He never said he wanted to buy our vineyard."

"There's a couple of reasons. First of all, excluding any violent act of nature, he'll make money from your wine sales. And at the going interest rate this investment will make more money for him than if it sat in the bank. And most important to Blackford is to keep the small family vineyards going." He turned to Ellie. "He's also agreed to keep this business transaction private."

Ellie knew that losing half of the income from their wine would hurt, and they wouldn't be able to pay all their workers. "What about the—?"

"The workers?" He interrupted her. "According to my numbers, you should be able to keep your regular employees. It'll work out, Ellie." He handed her the spreadsheet. "Without the large loan payments the money from the orchard, the cottages and the special events should be enough so you'll be able to have a comfortable life."

It looked great on paper, Ellie thought. "Is Henry still willing to keep our agreement to use his winery?"

"If you want. Although this could change somewhat." He turned to her grandfather. "After that five-year period, your vineyard will be yours once again. Now, you and Ellie have a couple of options here. Henry needs to update his equipment, and he wants to enlarge his winery production. For that he needs a larger winery. He would like to keep the same agreement he's had with the Irish Rogue label."

Her heart was pounding. She hated to be selfish, since she'd gotten her vineyard back. But her dream… She'd already lost the most important one. She glanced at Hugh. The winery was all she had left.

"What's the other option, Hugh?" Cullan asked.

His gaze went to Ellie as he leaned back in the chair. "Build your own winery."

Her heart raced. "But how can we afford it? We can't go into such debt again."

Hugh's gaze never wavered. "You take on another partner."

She sighed. "Who would want to invest…? Oh, no. Not McCutcheon. I won't have your father…"

"Not my father," he corrected. "Me. I want to invest in the winery."

"You? You know nothing about the wine business."

"I know the production end. I looked over the vineyard's profits for the last five years. It's a solid company…well run. Why wouldn't I want to invest?"

Ellie couldn't do this. Didn't he know how much it would hurt her to work with him, knowing they would never be together?

She looked at Papa. "You do what you want."

"No, Ellie. I can't do anything without your okay. In fact I'm signing the vineyard over to you. It's always been yours anyway. And any decision about what happens to it is yours, too."

"Thank you, Papa." She turned back to Hugh. "I want to thank you for all that you've done. And, yes, I'll accept Henry's offer for the vineyard. But…I'm sorry, Hugh, I can't let you invest in the winery."

She stood, and with the last of her composure she made it out the door. By the time she made it to her refuge, the vineyard, the tears were already falling.

Normally Hugh didn't give up so easily, but this time his heart wasn't in the fight. Ellie had made it clear. She didn't want him anywhere around her, whether it be business or personal.

"I'm sorry, Hugh," Cullan said. "She's been under a lot of stress lately."

"And she can't forgive me. She thinks I used her."

"Her feelings run deep." The older man stood. "She cares for you."

Hugh hadn't realized her rejection would hurt so much. "Oh, yeah, I can tell. She can't stand to be in the same room with me."

"Then tell her how you feel… Tell her why you really want to be her partner."

In the beginning he wouldn't even admit it to himself. But he wanted Ellie, wanted a future with her. "So she can throw it back in my face?"

"No, so she knows the truth." He placed his hand on Hugh's arm. "I know my granddaughter. Do you think if she didn't care she would raise such a ruckus?"

Hugh didn't know what to think. He was in love with Ellie Flanagan, but he couldn't make her feel the same way. Yet, if he didn't try to tell her… "Where is she?"

"My bet is she's up on the hill, probably talking to her grandmother." Cullan frowned. "She's lost a lot of people in her life… and she thinks she's lost you, too. Go to her," he said, giving him a nudge. "I'll have one of the workers put your things in the cottage."

"So you think I'm staying around?"

"I know you are, lad. For a long time."

Ellie stood, overlooking the vineyard. She wanted to push everything out of her head and just feel grateful to Henry Blackford for helping save Emerald Vale. But it wasn't the vineyard that was on her mind now.

She wondered if Hugh had left yet. Was he gone for good? After what she'd said to him she wouldn't blame him. She brushed away a wayward tear. She didn't need him anyway. Papa was here for her. And someday she'd build a winery. Why didn't that dream satisfy her any more?

"Ellie…"

She jerked around to see Hugh. She tried to draw a breath, but her chest was too tight.

"What are you doing here?"

He came closer. "Because of you. I'm here because of you."

"Please…Hugh. We said everything…"

"Not everything. At least let me tell you that I had no idea my father would show up that night. Also know that I wouldn't push your grandfather into selling. I didn't want him to have to sell Emerald Vale. I'd already approached Henry Blackford about the deal…two weeks ago."

Her eyes widened, but she couldn't speak.

"I no longer work for the McCutcheon Corporation. I resigned when I returned to San Francisco. So you see, Ellie, I wouldn't have been involved in the deal anyway."

"But what about you and your father?"

"Father, huh?" He chuckled. "Funny thing is, I never had a father growing up. I tried for a lot of years. I even went to work for him. But that didn't work, either. Worse, I realized I was turning into the same selfish man. I found I didn't like myself very much." He shrugged. "And I still didn't get my father's attention."

"Oh, Hugh, I'm sorry."

He shook his head. "It's okay, Ellie. You can't miss what you've never had. Or that's what I thought. Then I met you and Cullan and saw what a family truly was. As bad as things had gotten, Ellie, you and Cullan hung together. You would have survived anything because you had each other." His eyes met hers. "I envied that. For a time, I thought I could fit in here. You were quickly becoming my dream."

"Hugh."

"Let me finish. At first I never thought I'd want all this. It was the big city…the big job." He glanced around, then back at her. "Now I want all this. But only with you. From the first moment I saw you, you took my breath away. You were so beautiful. Your grandfather saw it, too. He said he felt the same way about his Eleanor." He reached for her and drew her closer.

"I love you, Ellie Flanagan. I want to share your dreams and build a life with you."

Her heart soared and she began to tremble. "I love you, Hugh. I'm sorry—"

He covered her mouth with a kiss that quickly had her aching for him. He finally released her. He grinned. "Say it again."

She smiled. "Oh, Hugh, I love you."

He picked her up in his arms and kissed her again and again. "Wait a minute. I just realized that I don't have a job. Do you know of anyone who needs a business analyst?"

She doubted that he was broke. "Yes, I just happen to know someone. Please, Hugh, you could work for Emerald Vale Orchard and Irish Rogue Vineyard…soon to be winery." She smiled. "You told me you're good with numbers."

"That's not all I'm good with." He captured her mouth in a searing kiss, giving her a sample.

Business could wait. There were more important things to deal with…like a future together.

EPILOGUE

IT WAS early summer in the vineyard. The rose garden was in full bloom, with a rainbow of color. White chairs had been set up on either side of the aisle that the bride would walk down to a flower-covered archway…and her groom.

Ellie stood in the back behind a screen. She was wearing her grandmother's wedding dress: antique white lace draped over a satin fitted gown that ended with a long train trimmed with tiny pearls. Her hair was pulled back and woven with fresh flowers attached to an elbow-length veil.

She drew another breath and turned to her grandfather. He looked handsome in his dark tuxedo.

"You look as beautiful as when I saw your grandmother on our wedding day." Tears filled his blue eyes. "She would be so happy you wore her dress."

"I couldn't wear anything else on my special day."

Their eyes met, and she wanted to say so many things, but realized he already knew them. "I love you, Papa."

"I love you, too, lass," he told her. "I hate giving you away today, but I know Hugh is a good man." His smile widened. "And I'll be waiting for those great-grandkids. Be happy, Ellie."

"I plan to, Papa."

The music changed, giving them their cue to begin. They stepped out onto the runner and started down the aisle. Ellie smiled as she saw all her friends and neighbors gathered there. Even Hugh's father was in attendance today.

Mac and his son had worked through some problems over the last months. They might never be close, but maybe they could be friends.

She gripped her bouquet of pink roses and raised her gaze to the man standing under the arbor. Her heart raced, as it did every time she saw Hugh McCutcheon. He looked handsome in his tuxedo adorned with a pink rose on the lapel.

She loved him with all her heart. Maybe even from that first day months ago, when Hugh had first arrived at Emerald Vale. But they'd decided to wait before they wed. It had given them time to work together and learn about each other. They'd even fought, and the making up had been wonderful. They had survived the remodeling of her parents' home, where they planned to begin their lives together…and start their own family.

Smiling, she reached the front of the garden. Her grandfather gave her a kiss, then gave her hand to Hugh. "Cherish her, son."

"I already do," Hugh said, and his eyes were on her. "You're so beautiful."

They turned to the priest.

The ceremony lasted a short time, and then came congratulations from well-wishers. The party moved on to the tables set up for the reception and dancing. It wasn't until hours later that they said their goodbyes to their guests and headed to the cottage. Tomorrow they would leave on their honeymoon—a week in Hawaii.

Hugh swung his bride into his arms and carried her over the threshold, inside the beautifully decorated room. There were flowers and lit candles everywhere.

"Oh, Hugh, it's so…romantic." He set her down. "Did you do this?"

"It was my idea, but Jillian helped me."

She frowned. "Should I be jealous?"

"Not in the least, Ellie Flanagan McCutcheon." He came to

her and kissed her, long and deep. Then with his bride in his arms he began to dance to the soft music that filled the room. "I'm glad we're alone," he whispered against her ear.

She looked at him. "So am I."

"I'll always remember the time I danced with you at the Stewart party. That was the first time I dreamed about us sharing our lives together."

They'd come a long way in just a few months. The bank loan was paid off, and Henry Blackford had pretty much left the operation as before. One good thing about the years Hugh had worked for his father: he'd made a lot of money. Money he'd invested wisely. Now they'd start making plans for the new Irish Rogue Winery.

"We're going to share a lot more," he told her. "We're building something for future generations." He kissed her. "A place that will always have love…and family. We're not just partners in business, but in life."

"Oh, my. I guess I can't call you the Hatchet Man anymore." Her arms tightened around his neck. "You're the Family Man now."

"Sounds wonderful to me." Hugh suddenly realized that after all the years he'd been searching he was home. With Ellie.

* * * * *

LIZ FIELDING

Chosen as the Sheikh's Wife

Liz Fielding was born with itchy feet. She made it to Zambia before her twenty-first birthday and, gathering her own special hero and a couple of children on the way, lived in Botswana, Kenya and Bahrain—with pauses for sightseeing pretty much everywhere in between.

She finally came to a full stop in a tiny Welsh village cradled by misty hills, and these days—mostly—leaves her pen to do the traveling.

When she's not sorting out the lives and loves of her characters, she potters in the garden, reads her favourite authors and spends a lot of time wondering, *What if….*

For news of upcoming books—and to sign up for her occasional newsletter—visit Liz's website at www.lizfielding.com.

CHAPTER ONE

VIOLET had been waiting for what seemed like hours, but eventually it was her turn and she limped forward with the object she'd brought along to the *Trash or Treasure* roadshow.

She'd already been through the junk/interesting/wow! "triage" at the entrance, and since the object she'd brought along for assessment had received a unanimous "wow!", and been red-stickered to indicate its status, a television camera zoomed in to film the expert's reaction.

She was not carried away on a tide of excitement by all this enthusiasm. It only meant that her piece of "trash" was unusual enough to arouse interest—and not necessarily of the kindly variety. This show was, after all, primarily entertainment, and if you set yourself up as an Aunt Sally, you had to expect the knocks.

She hadn't wanted to come. It was Sarah, her next-door neighbour, who'd insisted on dragging her reluctant bones along to the town hall so that she could be publicly humiliated for the amusement of several million viewers. Sarah who, just at the moment when she'd needed her for moral support, had disappeared in search of a loo.

Pregnancy was no excuse…

'What have we got here?' The "expert"—permanently tanned, silver-haired, a darling of the blue-rinse brigade—was familiar from the many evenings she'd sat watching this programme with her grandmother.

'I don't know,' she said truthfully, putting the brown padded envelope she had been clutching to her chest on the baize-covered table in front of him. 'To be honest I feel a bit of a fool bringing it here—' She felt better for getting that out, disassociating herself from any pretence to have found "treasure" '—but my neighbour lived in the Middle East for a while and she thought it was…interesting.'

Oh, lame, Violet Hamilton. Pathetic to blame someone not here to defend herself.

'Well, let's have a look at it, shall we?' He tipped a rag-wrapped bundle out onto the table in front of him.

'That's just how I found it,' Violet said quickly, not wanting him to think she routinely kept her valuables wrapped in rotted black silk. Not that she had any valuables. 'This morning,' she added. 'When I put my foot through the floorboards.' The cameraman pointed his lens at her strapped up ankle. Terrific… This was her "fifteen minutes of fame", and already her ankle was more interesting. 'It must have been there for years,' she said.

Without a word he carefully unfolded the rotted silk to reveal an ornately decorated dagger. Around them people crowded in to get a closer look.

That it was old was not in doubt. The handle had the patina of hard use, and inset in the top was a large, smoothly polished red stone the size of a pigeon's egg. The sheath wasn't straight but sharply curved and adorned with fancy silver and gold–coloured filigree work into which were set three similar tear-shaped red stones, decreasing in size as they reached the curved point and looking for all the world as if the stone on the handle was bleeding along its length.

The man said nothing for so long that Violet said, 'If I'd seen it on a market stall I'd have sworn it was a pantomime prop. Something the genie might wear in Aladdin.' The crowd, obligingly, laughed. 'All glass beads and plastic handle,' she added.

Then, as he eased the knife out of the sheath and the lights glinted off the blade, the laughter died.

'It's not a theatrical prop,' he said, unnecessarily.

'No.' And belatedly Violet wondered exactly how many laws she'd broken simply by carrying the thing in public.

'You found it under the floorboards, you said?' he prompted, with a keen, assessing glance. 'And which floorboards would they be?'

'*My* floorboards,' she replied a touch defensively, although now that the equity release people had done their sums the floorboards—along with most of the structure—were apparently theirs.

'I'm the fourth generation of my family to live there,' she added. And the last.

'Then it's likely that someone in your family hid it?'

'Unless burglars have started breaking in and leaving loot instead of taking it,' she agreed, and raised another laugh from the people crowded round to listen to what he had to say. Maybe she should consider a career in stand-up…

'Indeed,' he agreed, his smile as fake as his tan. It was *his* job to make the humorous remarks. 'Maybe we can come back to that.' Then, turning back to the knife, 'The Arab world has always been famous for its weapons and this is a *khanjar*, mostly worn now as a ceremonial piece in the same way as swords are worn with dress uniforms.'

He talked about the blade, about how the sharply curved scabbard was made, the skills being passed on from one generation of craftsmen to the next. He knew his stuff and the crowd around them was quiet now, intent. They knew that when he took this amount of time it was because he'd found something a bit special.

'This knife is exceptional,' he continued. 'Not only is the blade of the very highest quality, but the handle is made from rare, much-prized rhino horn.'

'Eeeuw…' Violet sat back, instinctively distancing herself from it.

'It's more than a hundred years old,' he said reassuringly.

'Does that make a difference?' she asked. 'The rhino still died just to furnish some man with a handle for his knife.'

'The transference of power had a potent appeal. It was a different world…'

'Not that different.'

'No.' Then, turning to a safer subject, he went on, 'The filigree work is fine gold and silver, and the use of rubies—'

'Rubies!' Violet exclaimed, forgetting all about the poor rhino who'd given up his horn just so that some dumb man would feel invincible when he wielded this blade. Forgetting everything in her shock. 'They can't possibly be rubies!'

This time his smile was genuine. It was finds like this, reactions like hers, that made the programme compulsive viewing.

'I mean, they're huge,' she said. Then, 'I thought they were glass.' And raised another laugh. This time for her foolishness. Everyone was an expert…

'They might well have been,' he agreed. 'All kinds of decoration can and have been used on this kind of knife, but these stones are the real thing. Cabochon rubies—that is they have been polished rather than cut.'

Violet, aware that something more was expected, could only manage a slightly croaky, 'Oh…'

Rubies…

'What we have here is the kind of weapon that would have been owned and worn by a chief. A sheikh,' he elaborated. 'Maybe even a sultan. It needs cleaning, of course, but even in this state I can't remember when I've seen anything quite so fine.'

It was rare for anything to reduce Violet to silence, but he had managed it.

'The really interesting question is how it came to be hidden beneath your floorboards.'

Violet was well aware what it must look like. What everyone must be thinking. That it had been stolen and, too hot to fence, had been hidden away and eventually forgotten about. But her family had enough of a history without adding larceny to the list, so she said, 'I suppose it could have something to do with the family legend.'

'Family legend?'

'The one about my great-great-grandmother being an Arabian princess who sewed her jewels into her clothes,' she said, 'and ran away from her husband with my great-great-grandfather.'

It was, gratifyingly, Mr Smooth's turn to be reduced to silence—if only momentarily.

'An Arabian princess?' he repeated, with a touch of uncertainty. She could see from his expression that he wasn't sure whether she was pulling his leg.

'With blue eyes,' she added, beginning to see the possibilities for entertainment herself. 'I'd always assumed it was just one of those tales that had grown in the telling.' She shrugged, leaving him to make up his own mind.

'Most stories have some element of truth in them,' he suggested. 'Was he a soldier? Your great-great-grandfather?'

'He was in the army. He was a medic. Stretcher-bearer,' she explained.

'Quite.' Then, 'It's more likely that he brought this back from the Middle East as a trophy,' he said, apparently discounting the Arabian princess theory as pure fantasy. 'Possibly from Turkey. This kind of elaborate decoration was favoured in the Ottoman dynasty.'

'Actually,' she said, refusing to allow him to dismiss her story in quite so casual a manner, 'it was the princess and the jewels I always assumed were the tall stories.' Her great-great-grandfather had braved artillery fire to carry wounded soldiers to safety, had a Military Medal to attest to his heroism, and she wasn't having him publicly branded a thief. 'Great-Great-Grandma Fatima was real enough. I have a photograph of her.'

There was a stiffly posed sepia-tinted photograph of a tall, exotically handsome woman, standing behind her seated husband, in the "family gallery" on the kitchen dresser.

'And a letter. In Arabic…'

'Well…' For a moment he appeared lost for words—twice in one day had to be a record. 'Well, you have a real story. And a rich treasure. Knives like these are very much in demand, and if you were to put it up for auction in a specialist sale…'

He mentioned some ridiculous sum of money, and all around her she heard gasps. And she was the one left struggling for words.

It was, Violet thought, numbly, a bit like a fairy tale.

She'd been in her late grandmother's bedroom, emptying her wardrobe, sorting out what was good enough to send to the charity shop, when she'd stepped back and gone through a floorboard that had creaked for as long as she could remember. And then, having pulled out her foot, she'd seen the carefully wrapped black silk bundle.

Buried treasure.

She was still in shock when the photographer from the local newspaper said, 'Smile!' and took her photograph.

'I'm sorry to disturb you, Fayad,' the ambassador said, but the press attaché has just received a call from the news desk of the *London Chronicle* about a story they're running tomorrow. It's something I thought you might want to know about.'

Sheikh Fayad al Kuwani, grandson to the ruler of Ras al Kawi, looked up from his laptop. His cousin would not have disturbed him unless it was something important.

'What scandal has my father visited upon us now?' he asked, sitting back, prepared for the worst.

'No… No, it's nothing like that, *in sh'Allah*,' Hamad was quick to reassure him. 'It seems that a young woman took a spectacular *khanjar* for expert valuation to some television programme that was being recorded this afternoon.'

'That makes the national news in this country?'

'There were rubies,' he replied. 'Very large rubies. And a story about a runaway Arabian princess and stolen jewels, which apparently makes it…' He hesitated, then with distaste, said, 'Sexy.'

Fayad stilled. 'Go on.'

'The local paper picked up the story and passed it along, and, having done some research, the *Chronicle* has inevitably come up with the mystery of the long-lost Blood of Tariq. They're running the story using the photograph of your great-great-grandfather with Lawrence, along with the original 1917 despatch from the front line in tomorrow's first edition. They were hoping for a comment from the embassy.'

'Did they get one?'

'Only that many fakes of the Blood of Tariq had been produced over the years, and this is undoubtedly one of them. That the value of the rubies is nothing compared to the value of owning the *khanjar* touched by Lawrence.'

'Yes…' Fayad sat back, squeezing the bridge of his nose between his fingers.

The Blood of Tariq had a mystical power that put it beyond price. To hold it, possess it, was to hold the fate of Ras al Kawi in your hand.

A fake.

It had to be a fake. But in the present climate that might be irrelevant.

It was what people believed that mattered.

Lost, the *khanjar* was a legend, a tale for old men as they sat around the campfire recalling past glories.

Found, it was trouble.

His grandfather was failing in health, his father was a disaster, and in the wrong hands even a fake, especially one with such an incendiary story attached to it, could prove disastrous to his country.

'You know who she is, this woman? Where to find her?'

'Her name is Violet Hamilton. She's twenty-two years old, unmarried. For the last three years she's been caring for her sick grandmother. The old lady died two weeks ago. At present she's living alone in her grandmother's house in Camden, where the *khanjar* was found. The equity of the house is owned by a property company, however, so she is about to become homeless.'

Fayad raised an eyebrow and the ambassador smiled. 'I don't ask how he does it, but in any exchange of information you can be sure that our man came out with the better deal.'

'Thank him for me.'

'I will.' Then, 'You'll make her an offer for it? You know it can't be real, Fayad. The original was surely broken up for the gold, the stones, decades ago.'

'Princess Fatima would never have done that. She knew that its worth lay in more than rubies and gold. Knew its power in the right hands. But, real or fake, it's a bad time for it to come to light. There are tribal factions who will move heaven and earth to get hold of it.'

Because of the reclusive nature of his grandfather, and the lack of interest his father had shown in anything but money, Ras al Kawi had remained relatively untouched by the tide of offshore banking and tourism that had swept through neighbouring countries.

Fayad had such plans for it, and now, just when things were finally beginning to take shape and he was preparing to move the country into the twenty-first century, onto the international stage, he was being faced with some mystical symbol straight out of a medieval melodrama.

It couldn't just be coincidence.

This had to be some elaborate hoax set up by someone planning to seize power. Except for the story of the runaway princess. And yet, for power, some disaffected member of the family might have betrayed them. Even his disinherited father…

'It scarcely matters if it is real or not, Hamad,' he said abruptly. 'We have to secure this knife before the story gains ground. And the woman, too.'

'The woman? You're not suggesting you carry her back to Ras al Kawi as symbolic proof of the restoration of Kuwani pride? As your grandfather's ambassador, I really could not allow that.'

'As my grandfather's ambassador I suggest you concentrate on the word "symbolic". Forget the *khanjar* for a moment. How safe do you think Miss Hamilton will be once it becomes rumoured that she is a descendant of Princess Fatima? There will be people ready to use her as a cipher at best. At worst...' He left that to his cousin's imagination.

'And you? What do you want with her, Fayad? Bearing in mind that I will be the one carpeted by the British Foreign Secretary if anything should happen to her.'

'What could I possibly want other than to extend to this descendant of Princess Fatima the hospitality of our country?' he replied wryly. 'Invite her to discover her true heritage.'

Hamad gave him a look that suggested he could think of any number of things, but confined himself to, 'And suppose she doesn't want to go to Ras al Kawi?'

'I will have to use all my diplomatic skills to persuade her that it's in her best interests. Have no fear, Hamad. She will be treated with the utmost respect.' Then, almost as an afterthought, 'After all, if she genuinely is a descendant of Fatima al Sayyid, then she, too, is a princess.'

'In other words she'll be fêted and entertained and never notice that she's in a gilded cage. What happens when she wants to fly?'

'My grandfather is desperate for me to remarry,' he said, without expression. 'An alliance between the Kuwani family and a descendant of Princess Fatima al Sayyid would be right in so many ways...'

'The Sayyid family might not take that view. Nor might Miss Hamilton.'

'True. But possession, as they say, is nine-tenths of the law.'

'You haven't got her yet, Fayad. For all you know she's already sold the *khanjar* to one of the dealers who undoubtedly take a keen interest in these events.'

CHAPTER TWO

'HONESTLY, Violet,' Sarah said, shaking her head, 'that's the first place a burglar is going to look for valuables.'

'Then good luck to them.'

She'd wrapped the jewelled knife, still in its silk bundle, first in bubble wrap, then several layers of kitchen foil, and now, having carefully labelled it "chicken thighs", was busy chipping out enough space in the thickly frosted freezer compartment of her ancient fridge so that she could jam it in behind the defrosted bag of peas that she'd used as a compress on her ankle to bring down the swelling.

'As I know to my cost, an hour from now any burglar is going to need a blowtorch to get past the peas.'

'What if someone decides to steal the fridge?'

'Oh, please! You've only to listen to it to know that it's on its last legs,' she said, looking around at a kitchen that hadn't seen more than a change of wallpaper since the Formica revolution in the fifties. 'Like just about everything else in here.' She was going to miss it all so much… Then, because nothing, after all, had changed—she'd always known she'd have to leave, she grinned and said, 'I mean, who would be that desperate? But don't worry. I'll hack it out and take it to the bank tomorrow.'

'If I were you I'd cut out the middle man and take it straight to a dealer. Give that expert a call—he'll know someone reputable. He gave you his card, didn't he?'

She nodded.

'Well, there you are. Sorted. It'll make a decent deposit on a two-bedroom flat, and if you let a room you'll have the mortgage covered. You could finish that design course you were taking…'

'Get real, Sarah. Who in their right mind would give me a mortgage on the chance of me letting a room? Besides…' She shrugged, shook her head.

'What?'

'She stole it, didn't she? Okay, the jewels may have been technically hers, but the knife…'

'Violet, sweetheart. It was nearly a hundred years ago. Who are you going to give it back to?' She shook her head and Sarah frowned. 'Are you going to be all right?'

'Yes. Yes, of course I am,' she said, making an effort to pull herself together. 'I guess I'm still in a state of shock.'

'I'm not surprised. I thought the knife would be worth a bit, but that was an amazing result.'

'Yes.' That kind of amazing just made her feel uneasy. 'Thanks for insisting on dragging me along to the T or T roadshow today.'

'Oh, I just wanted to get on the telly. Trust me to miss the big moment. Never mind. I'll get a thrill out of watching you when the programme is broadcast next week.'

Violet pulled a face, hating the thought. 'I must have been mad to sign the release form.'

'It would have made no difference. You'll be front page news in the local paper tomorrow.'

This time she just groaned. 'What on earth made me say all that stuff about Great-Great Grandma Fatima? I must have been mad.'

'Was it true? Really?'

'You think I could make up something like that?' She nodded at the pictorial family gallery that her grandma had always kept on the dresser. 'That's her, at the top in the middle.'

'Goodness.' Sarah took the picture down to take a closer

look. 'You've got a look of her, Violet. Something about the eyes. Hers are light, too. That's strange, isn't it?'

'I suppose…'

Sarah put the picture back. 'I'd better get home and feed the brute before he chews through the table-leg.' She stopped in the doorway, pausing to look back. 'You will be careful, won't you, Violet? Once this gets out… Well, a woman with a nice little windfall is likely to find herself the target of all kinds of smooth-talking men looking for a soft touch.'

More likely find herself the target for every local villain, she thought.

Then, realising that Sarah was waiting for an answer, she laughed. 'You mean I might get a life?'

'And not before time. You've spent the last three years as a full-time carer. No holidays, scarcely a break. Nothing in your pocket but your carer's allowance and the little bit of money you make on your stall. Believe me, I know how hard it's been.'

'You're wrong, Sarah. It hasn't been hard. My grandmother was the one person in the entire world who was always there for me, who never let me down, and I loved her. I'm trying to tell myself that she isn't suffering anymore, but what's really hard is not having her here.'

Sarah gave her a hug, then, leaning back, said, 'You're so vulnerable just now. I'm afraid you're going to lose that tender heart to the first man you meet with a killer smile.'

'Chance would be a fine thing,' she said. 'Getting a life is going to have to wait a while. There's a ton of stuff to do here first. I've got to sort out Grandma's things. Find somewhere to live…'—the finance people had given her until the end of the month—'…and get a job.'

'Well, at least now you'll have some money behind you.'

'Yes…' Then, 'Thanks again for rushing to the rescue this morning.'

'Any time. Just scream.' Sarah grinned, hugged her again, and finally left.

Violet closed the door and leaned back on it for a moment.

Much as she loved Sarah, it was a relief to be on her own for a moment, to be able to think.

Could it possibly be true? About the exotic Fatima being a princess? She'd dismissed the idea as nonsense when Sarah had asked her, but was it? Really?

The TV expert had said the knife could have belonged to a sheikh or sultan, and it was worth a great deal of money. So why had she kept it? Hidden it beneath the floorboards when, presumably, her jewellery—according to family legend—had been sold to fund the purchase of this house?

As if it were too important, too precious, to part with? Hidden it and never told a living soul. Because if she had someone would have sold it long ago. If her grandma had known about it she wouldn't have sacrificed the house to raise money when she'd needed it. Would have passed on the secret when she knew she was dying…

She sighed. She didn't need more questions. It was answers she wanted. And upstairs, in the bottom of her gran's wardrobe, was an old Gladstone bag, stuffed with the kind of stuff that women couldn't part with. Dried flowers. Letters. Embroidered handkerchiefs. Bits of lace and ribbon. Wedding invitations, school reports—whoever would want to keep those!—theatre programmes. Greetings cards for every possible occasion. Great-Great-Grandad's Military Medal.

Generations of the stuff.

There had been a time, when she was a little girl, when it had been a magic bag, and being allowed to "tidy" it had been a special treat.

Then it had become an emotional ambush to be avoided at all costs. Full of things that just to look at, hold, brought tears welling to the surface: a postcard from her mother on honeymoon in Venice; a Mother's Day card she'd made when she was so little she'd needed her gran to help with the letters; a button from her father's jacket that she'd hidden there.

At the bottom, hidden by a false base, was the big envelope that she had not been allowed to open. The one containing family documents. The certificates—birth, marriage, death—that said who they were, where they came from. An envelope that her grandma had said she could open "when she was older".

Except, of course, the temptation had been too much for a curious ten-year-old. Which was how she knew about the Arabic letter, although at the time she hadn't realised what it was. How she knew why her grandmother had had to raise money in such a hurry…

She had a new document to add to the family archive, but she'd been putting it off. She'd been ignoring the bag ever since her grandmother had died, delaying the moment when she became the family matriarch. The keeper of its history. Its awful secrets.

Now she needed the letter from Fatima—there was an Iraqi woman who worked in the market who might be able to translate it for her—but she couldn't bring herself to simply dump the contents of the bag on her grandmother's bed.

It was not just the trivia of their lives, but the small tokens of love and remembrance that women clung to. Family history was written in the names of men, but this bag contained the women's story. In cards, tiny treasures, a crumbling corsage worn by some unknown girl with her heart full of hope.

It was only when the hall clock struck one that she realised how long she'd spent reading old letters, scanning cards that had nothing to do with her hunt for the truth about Fatima but everything to do with her life.

Her mother's life.

A school exercise book full of gold stars. An old blue passport. School photographs full of hope and promise that was never realised.

She put them to one side and pulled out the envelope. The certificates were all in there. And the letter written in flowing Arabic script that made her heart beat faster just to hold it. Only Fatima herself could have written it and she held it close to her heart as if she could feel the words, make some direct connection with this extraordinary woman.

She did not open the last envelope. The one containing the equity release documents that her grandmother had signed and the letter from her father.

Being old enough made no difference, and, as she had done when she'd defied her grandmother's ruling and opened it, she crawled into bed, pulling the ancient quilt over her. Except that this time there was no one to come and find her and comfort her.

It was the phone that woke her. Dragging her from somewhere so deep that she was certain that it must have been ringing for some time.

She ignored it and finally it stopped, allowing her to concentrate on her headache, and the fact that her eyes felt as if someone had been shovelling grit in them all night.

The bright sunshine didn't help.

With her hand shading her eyes, she made it to the bathroom. She was in the shower when the phone began to ring again. Sarah, she thought. It would be Sarah, worrying about her. She'd call her back…

She washed her hair, brushed her teeth. Decided to forget about getting dressed until she'd had coffee.

The local newspaper was lying on the mat. Her gran had liked her to read the local news to her…

She bent to pick it up, groaning as the headache she thought she'd defeated slid forward and collided with the back of her aching eyes.

Then she groaned again as she saw the front page. It must be a slow news day, because she seemed to fill the front page, staring like a rabbit caught in the media headlights, with the *Trash or Treasure* expert beside her displaying the *khanjar*. In full colour.

The headline read: ARABIAN 'PRINCESS' AT ROADSHOW.

What?

The doorbell rang and without thinking she wrenched the door open, certain that it would be Sarah. She'd taken to dropping in every morning over the last few weeks, to see if she needed anything. She usually came round the back, letting herself in with her "good neighbour" key, as she had yesterday when she'd heard her cry for help when the floor had given way.

Clearly the fact that the phone had gone unanswered was causing her concern, but since she'd bolted the back door last night the key would be useless.

But it wasn't Sarah, who was tiny—apart from around the middle, where she was spreading spectacularly—and fair; the figure that filled the tiny porch was her opposite in every conceivable way.

Tall, spare, broad-shouldered, male, there was nothing soft about him. His features were austere, chiselled to the bone, and his olive-toned skin was positively Mediterranean against a snowy band-collared shirt, fastened to the neck. His hair was thick and crisply cut. But it was his eyes that held her.

Dark as midnight and just as dangerous.

He looked very…foreign.

He was also stunningly, knee-wobblingly handsome.

Violet was suitably stunned. And her knees dutifully wobbled.

Just her luck that she'd emerged from the shower pink of face, with her hair in its usual wet tangle, and with nothing between her and decency but a film of moisturiser and a faded pink bathrobe that could only be described as…functional.

'Miss Hamilton?'

Oh, and guess what…? He had a voice like melted chocolate, delicately flavoured with an exotic, barely there accent.

Whatever he was selling, she was buying it by the crate…

Except, of course, that he was far too expensively dressed to be a door-to-door salesman. She knew clothes. And what he was wearing did not come off a peg in the high street.

Oh, well. She was expecting a visit from a representative of the finance company to call any day, with the release papers for her to sign so that they could sell the house, recover their money.

This had to be him.

'Miss Violet Hamilton?' he repeated, when she didn't answer.

'Who?' she asked, just to hear him say Violet again. Long and slow.

Vi-o-let.

Pronouncing every syllable, turning a name she loathed only slightly less than the hideously shortened "Vi" into the most desirable name in the entire world.

'I'm looking for Miss Violet Hamilton.' And, taking the newspaper from her hand, he held the front page up for her to see. 'I believe I've found her.'

No point pretending to be the lodger, then. Asking him to come back when she'd gussied herself up, straightened her hair, applied some make-up, was decked out in one of her more creative outfits. Oh, well…

'And here I was kidding myself that the photograph is so awful that you couldn't possibly tell,' she said. 'Clearly I was fooling myself.'

He looked at the photograph and then at her, for rather longer than seemed necessary just to confirm the likeness. Then, clearly thinking better of commenting one way or the other, he returned the paper and said, 'I am Fayad al Kuwani, Miss Hamilton.' And he held out a visiting card—as if they couldn't be printed off by the dozen in any name you cared to dream up by anyone with a computer.

Except that this wasn't a do-it-yourself job, but embossed on heavy ivory-coloured card.

If he was from the finance company, he certainly wasn't one of the foot-soldiers.

The front of the card gave no hint, but contained only his name: *Fayad al Kuwani*. Unusual enough. She turned it over. The back was blank. No address, no phone number.

Obviously this was a man whose name was enough for those with the wit to recognise it. Which did not include her.

'Nice card,' she said. 'But a trifle shy of information.'

'The Ras al Kawi Embassy will vouch for me.'

'Oh, well, that's all right, then,' she said. Her friends would have recognised sarcasm. He apparently did not, but merely nodded. Good grief, he was serious…

Ras al Kawi? Where was that?

'I need to talk to you about a *khanjar* that I believe is in your possession,' he said. 'It is possible that it once belonged to my family.'

'Oh?' Then, realising that he'd come to demand it back, 'It's amazing how fast good news spreads.'

'You have no idea. Perhaps I should wait in my car while you…?'

He made the vaguest of gestures, resolutely looking at her face, avoiding her bare legs, the shabby bathrobe that had a tendency to gape at the neck. It made no difference. Every inch of her skin tingled.

'Dress?' she offered, lippy to the last. Except that the word didn't come out quite as she'd intended, but thick and throaty. More to avoid those eyes than because she was interested in his choice of transport, Violet looked past him.

A black Rolls-Royce was parked at the kerb. The little green and gold flag on the bonnet stirred in the breeze.

She barely stopped herself from letting slip an expression that would have brought her a rebuke from her grandma.

Her breathless, 'Who *are* you?' wasn't a whole heap better.

'If your story is true, Miss Hamilton, then your great-great-grandmother, Princess Fatima al Sayyid, was once married to my great-great-grandfather.'

At which point she did let slip a word that she used only under the most extreme pressure.

She would have been embarrassed about that, but a scream from rear of the house—Sarah's scream—obliterated the sound.

CHAPTER THREE

VIOLET didn't stop to consider what might have prompted the scream. All she could think was that Sarah was in trouble. But as she turned to rush to her aid, Fayad al Kuwani caught her arm, held her.

'Who is that?' he demanded. 'I understood you lived alone.'

'My neighbour. She's pregnant…' she said, shaking him off, leaving him with nothing but a handful of bathrobe. For a minute she didn't think he was going to let go, but even when it slid from her shoulder, exposing more of her than any man had ever seen, she didn't stop. She'd have run naked into hell for Sarah, and he must have realised that because before that happened he released her, uttering a muffled oath.

It wasn't in English, and she didn't wait for him to translate, but pulled her robe tightly back in place and raced down the hall.

She burst through the kitchen door to find Sarah, still clutching the newspaper she'd brought for Violet, standing on her doorstep. A man, stocking-masked, had his arm around her throat.

'The knife,' he said. 'I want the knife.'

Violet tried to speak, but her tongue was thick, her mouth dry. And, having come to an abrupt halt, she appeared to be fixed to the spot.

'Give it to me!' he demanded, tightening his grip on Sarah. 'Now!' His voice was shaking as much as his hands. Somehow knowing that he was scared, too, didn't help. Scared men were dangerous…

'It's in the fridge,' she managed, not wanting to make any sudden moves.

'Get it!'

'It's frozen. I'll need something to hack it out with.'

Why had that seemed such a good thing yesterday? Right now she'd have given anything to be able to just hand the wretched thing over if only Sarah was safe.

'Use your hands!'

She flew to the fridge, wondering if there was any chance of Mr Tall, Dark and Dangerous doing anything beyond sitting in the safety of his very expensive car and using an equally expensive cellphone to call the police. Well, you wouldn't want to get a suit like that messed up, would you?

Obviously people who flew flags on their cars got an instant response, but it wouldn't be quick enough to help, and if he took after his great-great-grandfather, she was beginning to understand why Fatima had run…

She opened the fridge door. The light, which had been flickering uncertainly for weeks, didn't come on, and it suddenly occurred to her that everything was deathly quiet.

For a moment it seemed as if the world had stopped spinning, then, as she opened the freezer compartment, icy water hit the floor and splashed up over her bare legs, and she was unable to hold back a shriek of her own. After that everything happened very fast. There was a dull thud, and then she was spun off her feet as someone rushed passed her and out through the front door.

Then, as she lay there, icy water seeping through her bathrobe, she had a grandstand view of Tall, Dark and Dangerous lowering Sarah, very gently, into the nearest chair.

Hero material after all.

'Violet!' Sarah exclaimed. 'Are you all right?'

'Me?' she replied, feeling a touch light-headed. 'I'm just peachy.' Then, as it all came rushing back to her, she scrambled to her feet. 'Forget me. What about you? Are you hurt? Is the baby okay?'

'I'm fine,' Sarah said, rubbing at her throat. 'Really. It all happened so fast…'

Her voice was as shaky as her brave smile, and Violet hugged her.

'I'll call the doctor. Get him to check you over.'

'There's no need. Honestly…'

'There's every need,' she said, picking up the telephone, hitting fast dial and asking the receptionist to get the doctor to drop everything and get over here right *now*.

'You shouldn't have done that, Violet,' Sarah protested. 'She's really busy.'

'I think it would be wise to take precautions,' their hero advised. Neither shaken nor stirred, his designer suit still immaculate, he was as steady as a rock, while Violet's legs went suddenly rubbery as reality hit her. She subsided in the chair beside Sarah.

'I wish I'd never seen that knife.'

Fayad, wishing something very similar, flexed his hand, using the pain to distract himself from the sight of Violet Hamilton's creamy shoulder. 'Maybe you should have the doctor check you over, too. You've had a nasty shock.'

'I'm fine,' she snapped. 'I thought you'd run out on me.' Then, tugging her robe back into place, 'Sorry.'

'Don't apologise. You distracted him while I came around the back. A much better plan.'

'I didn't have a—' She stopped as she realised that, somewhat unexpectedly, he was teasing her. 'You'd better run your hand under cold water before it swells.'

Maybe he looked as if he didn't know how to do that for himself, because she leapt to her feet, turned on the tap, filled a glass with cold water for her friend, then, taking his hand, held it under the running water.

'How does it feel?' she asked.

How did it feel to have this stunning girl leaning against

him, holding his hand? Her hair, her temple, inches from his mouth, an unconscious display of the soft curve of her breast as she bent closer to check the damage for herself.

She really didn't want to hear about that kind of emptiness.

When he didn't answer, she looked up at him with those extraordinary sea-coloured eyes. 'Maybe you should go to the hospital?' she suggested. 'In case you've broken something?'

'It's just a graze,' he assured her. 'I've had worse. My only regret is that I didn't hit him harder.'

'It doesn't matter. He's gone.' Then, as if suddenly conscious of their closeness, she stepped back, pulled her robe tighter, refastening the belt. 'Just leave it there for a moment,' she advised. 'To be on the safe side.'

'He's gone for now,' Fayad corrected, testing his hand, turning off the water. 'He'll be back. Or someone very like him.'

'Not if you take it away with you. The *khanjar*.' She returned to the fridge, fetched a foil-wrapped parcel and laid it on the table, as if she couldn't bear to hold it for longer than necessary. 'I hope it's okay.'

He unwrapped the foil, the bubble wrap, the black silk that was rotting at the folds, to reveal the knife. Deadly, beautiful beyond imagining. And trouble.

For both of them.

'I will, of course, relieve you of this burden,' he said. 'However, I'm afraid simply removing it to a place of safety is not likely to end the matter. You're a descendant of Fatima al Sayyid, a woman who ran from her husband, taking the Blood of Tariq with her.'

'The Blood of Tariq?'

'That's what they called it in the newspaper,' her friend said. She had now recovered her composure, along with her colour. 'You and your fancy piece of cutlery made the nationals, sweetie. It's got quite a history, apparently.'

'What kind of history?'

She looked not at her friend, but at him, and he said, 'My

great-great-grandfather, Tariq al Kuwani, was wounded fighting for Arab freedom against the Ottoman Empire in the First World War. Yours was there, too, I understand?'

'He was a medical orderly.'

'The bravest of men went into battle armed only with a stretcher.'

'Yes,' she said, finally finding a smile, and he knew he'd said the right thing. 'He was given a medal.' Then, 'Your great-great-grandfather was armed with this *khanjar*, I suppose?'

'I doubt the Blood of Tariq ever saw action. It's a showpiece, a symbol of wealth and power. A prize captured in battle that Lawrence placed in his hand, declaring that victory had been won with the blood of Tariq. Nonsense, of course, but great PR. And it became a potent symbol in my country.'

'So potent that someone would threaten a pregnant woman to get hold of it?' The smile had gone; her laugh was derisory. 'All that must have happened nearly a hundred years ago!' she protested.

She put on a good show, but there was no doubt that she was quaking to her bare toes.

'Excuse me,' her friend—Sarah—intervened. 'This is all very interesting, but isn't someone going to call the police?'

'I'm sorry you were caught up in this…Sarah?' She nodded. 'My car is outside. I would be happy to take you to the hospital.'

She waved away the suggestion. 'Honestly, I'm fine.' She had quickly regained her colour, and, apparently, her sense of humour. 'And it was my own stupid fault. When I came through the hedge and saw him forcing the door I just screamed.'

They both looked at the splintered doorframe.

'The bolt is only as good as the wood that was holding it,' Sarah said. 'Pathetic. If I'd kept my head I could have slipped home and called the police myself, but you just don't think, do you?'

'Oh, Sarah! I'm so sorry…'

'It wasn't your fault.'

'Of course it was. If I hadn't blabbed about the family history it wouldn't have been all over the newspapers.' Then, 'I'd have given him anything he asked for—you know that, don't you?'

'You were wonderful.' Then, regarding him with a frown, 'As for you—heroic is the only word for it. But where did you spring from? And why do I think I know you?'

'I was at the front door when you screamed, and since I was unable to prevent Miss Hamilton's heroic, if foolhardy, frontal assault, I came around the back.'

'The classic pincer movement.'

'Indeed.' Then, 'As to your second question, I think you'll find that my photograph is also on the front page of the newspaper you're holding.'

It had been brought to him the instant the first edition had hit the streets. The later editions of some of the other papers had picked it up, too.

'Oh, *right*,' Sarah said. 'That's why I was coming round. To show Violet,' she said, opening it up. 'As I said, you made the nationals. The Blood of Tariq appears to be some long-lost treasure.' Then, 'Oh, good grief…'

'What?' Violet demanded.

Sarah gestured in his direction. 'Listen to this. "A spokesman for Sheikh Fayad al Kuwani,"' she read, angling the front page so that Violet could see the headshot of him they'd found in their files.

They both looked at him, and he acknowledged the likeness with the slightest of bows. Sarah smiled. Violet did not.

Despite the damp, tousled hair, the appalling bathrobe, there was something intensely regal about her. The height helped, of course—she was tall for a woman—but she had a look that could, he suspected, quell the slightest familiarity.

'"…*Sheikh* Fayad al Kuwani,' her friend Sarah continued, emphasising his title, '"heir apparent to the throne of Ras al Kawi and a direct descendant of Tariq al Kuwani, who is in London this week for an energy conference, suggested that the *khanjar* might be one of a number of fakes that are known to be in existence…"'

Sarah held out the paper to Violet and, smiling, looked up at him. 'So? Is it a fake, Sheikh Fayad al Kuwani?'

He looked at Violet, then said, 'I think not.'

'She does have a look of her great-great-grandmother, doesn't she?'

'Excuse me?'

Sarah nodded at the dresser, and his heart almost stopped beating as he saw the photograph on the top shelf.

From the moment he'd set eyes on Violet Hamilton he'd been certain that she was a direct descendant of Princess Fatima. Ebony-black hair, skin so fair that it was almost luminous, and eyes the curious colour that was the legacy of Portuguese invaders, who had built their forts along the coast of Africa and the Gulf centuries earlier, told their own story.

But here was proof indeed—a face he recognised from his own generation of the Sayyid family. Boys he'd grown up with. Their mothers, aunts, sisters.

They were one of the great tribes of Ras al Kawi, equal in status, wealth, influence to the Kuwani, until Lawrence had singled out his great-great-grandfather and in one romantic gesture made him the rallying point for all the tribes of the region, placing him at the head of the newly formed nation of Ras al Kawi.

He reached up and took the photograph from the shelf, then turned to Violet Hamilton and, with the slightest of bows, said, 'Will you come to Ras al Kawi with me, Princess? Bring the *khanjar* home?'

CHAPTER FOUR

'PRINCESS! Oh, please…'

'The daughter of a sheikha is a sheikha. As a direct descendant of Fatima, the title is yours by right.'

She shook her head emphatically. 'No.'

'It's the truth, and I am inviting you to see for yourself where you come from, to learn your history. To return the Blood of Tariq and place it where it belongs, in the hand of my grandfather.' He glanced at her neighbour, then back at Violet. 'In Ras al Kawi I can offer protection from those who would stop at nothing to use you.'

Use her? How? She was nobody…

'I…I can't,' she said. 'I can't just up sticks and go to Ras al…'

'Kawi. Ras al Kawi.'

'Ras al Kawi.' She repeated the name as if it echoed, like some precious tribal memory, deep in her heart.

'If you are not here, they cannot use you. Or threaten your friends to get what they want.'

'They wouldn't!' she exclaimed. Then realised that they already had. 'What do they want?'

'Power,' he said.

'What about you, Sheikh Fayad?' she asked, apparently unimpressed. 'I don't know you. Are *you* using me?'

She looked at him as if she could see right through him. Remembering the way he'd spoken to his cousin about her, his utter disregard for her own wishes, his only concern with what was expedient for his country, that was not a comfortable thought.

It was, nonetheless, essential to convince her of his sincerity. But while some people were easily won round with smiles and charm, he sensed that this was not the way with Violet Hamilton. Some inner sense warned him that she would mistrust them.

'I understand your hesitation, Princess. No sensible woman would fly into the unknown with a stranger. What can I do to satisfy you that I mean you no harm? Whose word would you trust? The Mayor of London?' he suggested. 'I'm having lunch with him. Or maybe you'd prefer to have my character from the Foreign Secretary?'

'Go for the Prime Minister,' Sarah urged. 'If you can get him down here I'd really like a word with him about local schools.'

Violet simply regarded him with reproachful eyes, and he understood instantly that it had been a mistake to offer such people to vouch for his honour. As heir to a country with whom they wanted to do business, she knew they wouldn't hesitate to put his needs before that of some ordinary girl.

'Maybe you'd have more trust in the Englishwoman who was my son's nanny?' he offered.

'Why his nanny? Why not his mother?' she asked.

Inwardly, he flinched at the directness of her question. Outwardly, he allowed nothing to show.

'My son and his mother both died when he was no higher than my knee,' he replied.

Behind him, her friend caught her breath, and for a moment he thought he had Violet, too. It gave him no satisfaction. On the contrary, it felt like a tacky play for sympathy, something he neither deserved nor wanted, when all he wanted was her trust.

He was a diplomat, well used to dealing with awkward situations, using words to make things happen, and yet, confronted by this young woman wearing nothing but a shabby bathrobe, he appeared to have lost control of the situation. Of his thoughts. Of something more. Something that he didn't want to think about…

'I'm sorry,' she said. Her eyes were soft with genuine sympathy but her gaze was direct and, standing straight and tall, steel in her backbone, she said it again. 'I'm sorry, Sheikh Fayad al Kuwani. Take the Blood of Tariq to your grandfather, but I must stay here. I have to pack up the house. Clear everything…'

Without warning the steel buckled, and for the second time she grabbed for a chair as if, suddenly, the shock of what had just happened, the realisation of what was ahead, had drained the fight from her.

He caught her, lowered her into it, filled a glass with water and held it while she took a sip. Held it until her long, slender fingers stopped shaking sufficiently for her to take it safely.

'Stupid… Stupid…' she said.

'Don't be so hard on yourself. Your friend is not the only one who has had a shock, Princess.'

'Don't…' She shook her head. 'Don't call me that. It isn't right.'

'It is not only right, it is your heritage,' he said. And it was true. She did not need silk, jewels. It was in her manner, her bearing, some edge to her character…' Come to Ras al Kawi and you will see for yourself,' he urged.

'I can't. Truly. There's just too much to do here.'

'Her grandmother used a dodgy equity release scheme to raise some money on the house years ago,' Sarah explained. 'Before they were properly regulated. Now she's dead it's all theirs. Lock, stock and rotting floorboard. They want her out by the end of the month.'

So, it was as he'd been told. Violet Hamilton was without fortune, homeless, and yet she did not ask for money for the *khanjar*, nor grab at an invitation to be fêted as a princess.

'Where will you go?' he asked.

'It depends how much she gets for the *khanjar*,' Sarah replied, meaningfully.

'Stop it, Sarah. It's not mine to sell.' Then, gathering herself, 'If you'll excuse me, Sheikh Fayad, I have things to do.'

She meant it, he realised. Was immovable.

He wasn't used to being refused anything, wasn't prepared to accept defeat now, but continuing to press the matter would only intensify her resistance.

'Very well. If you insist on staying, I have no choice but to accept your decision.' He took a pen from his pocket. 'Give me the card.'

For a moment she looked as if she might resist, but then fished it out of her pocket.

He wrote a number on the back and returned it to her. 'I have to go now, but I will arrange for your door to be repaired. Someone will come before the end of the day. And if you should change your mind about coming to Ras al Kawi, you can reach me on that number day or night.' He handed it to her. Looked directly into her eyes. 'While I have a breath in my body my family will be at your command, Violet Hamilton. All you have to do is call.' Then he picked up the *khanjar*, bowed, slightly, and said, 'Princess… Sarah…' before turning and walking out through the still wide open front door.

Curious neighbours had gathered, but, looking neither to left nor right, he stepped into his car and, as it sped away from the kerb, began to make a series of phone calls.

'He might at least have said thank you,' Violet said, as the front door closed behind him. 'He just walked away, didn't look back.'

'They don't. It's their way. But they never forget a debt. And that "breath in my body" pledge is not meaningless. You will be paid one way or another.'

'I don't want to be paid,' she said, shaking her head. 'I'm just glad to be rid of the thing. Then, unable to help herself, she asked, 'What's it like, Sarah? Have you been there? Ras al Kawi?'

'We were next door in Ras al Hajar. The ruler there has an English wife. Did you know that? She used to be a foreign correspondent.' She sighed. 'Terrific place to live.' Then, 'Ras al Kawi is less developed, and the old Emir is a bit of a recluse. I always wanted to go there. It's mountainous, and has the most fabulous coastline.'

'It sounds lovely.'

'You're wishing you hadn't been so quick to turn him down now?'

'No. No, of course not.'

Sarah laughed, clearly not believing her. 'Violet, sweetheart, you remember me saying that you should be careful not to get swept off your feet by the first good-looking man that came your way?'

'I remember.' Not that she'd needed telling. With a father like hers, trust in the male did not come easily. Then, managing a grin, 'Did I do good?'

'Oh, you were faultless. You had the heir to a sheikhdom wanting to treat you like a princess and you were ice.' She shook her head as she got to her feet. 'No need to worry about you losing your head. If you can resist such a killer combination of cheekbones and tragedy you'll probably die an old maid.'

Sarah was joking. If only she knew… 'Are you saying I should have gone with him? Just like that?'

'You said you wanted a life.'

'I did. I do. But I was thinking of starting on the nursery slopes and working up to dangerous. Going with Sheikh Fayad would be like taking a ski-run down Mount Everest.' Then, because she might be regretting it just a little bit, and would rather not think about quite how much, 'That guy at the library keeps asking me out.'

'Really? Not so much nursery slopes as totally flat, then. You do know that he never goes anywhere without his mother?'

'I had heard she was a touch…possessive,' Violet replied, laughing despite everything. 'But just think how safe I'd be.'

'Oh, please. I didn't expect you to take me that literally. Life doesn't start small and build up in carefully managed steps to exciting. Exciting is so rare that you have to grab it when you get the chance. You've got a lot of catching up to do, and even if you did live to regret it at least you would have lived.'

'You've changed your tune!' Then, with those dangerously attractive blade-edged cheekbones of Sheikh Fayad, his thick dark hair, broad shoulders still a vivid memory, Violet said, 'So, to recap. Your advice is now to forget safe, go for excitement. Got it.' Then, 'So shall I pick up Molly from playgroup for you? Since you have to wait in for the doctor.'

Sarah laughed. 'Okay, I'll stop nagging. But you can't leave the house. In case you hadn't noticed, your back door is hanging off its hinges.'

'There's nothing to steal,' Violet pointed out, and propped it back in place. 'There. From the outside it'll look solid enough.'

Sarah went home to wait for the doctor. Violet dressed, then swiftly gathered up the scattered contents of the Gladstone bag, stuffing everything back inside, before returning it into the wardrobe.

Violet picked up Molly, stayed to have a sandwich with Sarah, then walked round the back, squeezing through the gap in the hedge. She thought she'd wedged the door firmly in its frame, but a gust of wind must have caught it, because it had fallen in.

Then she stepped inside.

Her kitchen was wrecked. Drawers pulled out, plates smashed. Photographs and china from the dresser trampled underfoot

And, in the middle of the kitchen, the fridge was lying on its side. If it hadn't been beyond repair before, it was now.

In shock, she walked through the house to discover that

every room had been given the same treatment. Even the precious treasures that had been stored through generations in the old leather bag had been tipped out, crushed beneath careless feet. Except for the envelopes. They were gone.

No one would call him while he was at a formal lunch, and normally Fayad would have switched off his cellphone. But he'd promised Violet Hamilton that he would be there if she needed him. And as the phone began to vibrate against his heart, he knew she needed him.

It could only be Violet, and with a brief apology to his host, he left the table.

'Princess?' He spoke without thinking. How easy it was to address her by that title. How right it felt.

'They came back…'

Her voice—little more than a tremor, barely audible—sent real fear coursing through his veins.

'Did they hurt you?' he asked, forcing himself to keep his voice low, when all he wanted to do was roar with fury. If they'd hurt her they'd pay for it.

He was already paying. He'd known the danger, had asked his aide to organise private security, but these things took time to put in place and his enemies hadn't waited.

The man who'd escaped had simply waited until he left, then called for reinforcements.

But an angry response wouldn't help Violet. She'd come through the first attack relatively unscathed, but now she was seriously frightened and she needed a calm response.

'Do you need medical help?' he asked, when she didn't reply.

'I wasn't here.' Then, on a sob, 'Please. Take me away…'

He uttered a prayer of thanks that she had been out of the house, that she'd chosen to call him, then said, 'I'll be with you in twenty minutes.'

He made it in fifteen and, ignoring the front door, went straight around the back. He took in the wreckage of the kitchen, the rest of the ground floor. Then sprinted up the stairs and found her, huddled against the head of a big, old-fashioned double bed, clutching an old leather bag to her chest.

The mess was indescribable. The wardrobe had been ransacked, its contents spilled on the floor. A lamp overturned and smashed.

Ignoring it, he climbed up beside her, put his arms around her and pulled her close, kissing the top of her head as if she were a child. For a moment she reacted like a wild thing, fighting him, lashing out in her anger and pain, but he held on, murmuring the soft words of comfort that his mother had poured into his own ears as a child.

She wouldn't understand them, but it wasn't the words that mattered. There was a tone of voice, a universal comfort that transcended language.

For a moment she was deaf to him, but then a great shudder went through her and, as she leaned into him, hot tears soaked through his jacket to his skin, scalding him with her pain.

He held her close, stayed with her while his staff, summoned as he was driven to her aid, arrived to pack her things, take charge here.

And all the time he held her his heart was singing, because she hadn't called her friend who was just next door. She'd called him. Had wanted him. Had trusted him.

'Princess?' he prompted, when a nod from his aide assured him that everything had been done. That his plane would be waiting by the time they arrived at the airport so that they could board without delay. 'Violet?'

She lifted her head as if the weight of it was almost too much to bear. Her face was ashen, her eyes grey with misery, her lashes clumped together with tears. And still she was beautiful.

'It's time to go,' he said.

She didn't ask where he was taking her, just nodded, and he stood up, helping her up, keeping his arm about her as she found her feet. After a moment, she took an unsteady step back. He reached out to stop her from falling, but she straightened.

'Sarah,' she said. 'I have to tell Sarah I'm leaving or she'll worry.'

'She's here.'

'Violet? I saw the car.' Then, with a gasp as she saw the mess, 'Why didn't you call me?'

'She was protecting you,' Fayad told her. 'Protecting your family.'

'Who will protect *her*?'

'I will.'

For a moment Sarah challenged him with a look then, apparently satisfied that he meant what he said, she took Violet in her arms and hugged her.

'I'm so sorry. This is all my fault. If I hadn't dragged you along to that wretched *Trash or Treasure* roadshow…'

'You didn't do this, Sarah,' Fayad said, handing her a card. 'You shouldn't have any more trouble. My people will be here, taking care of the house, and I've organised security, but if you're worried at any time, if you need anything, call this number. My cousin, Hamad al Kuwani, is the ambassador, and he knows who you are and will help in any way…'

'Thank you.' Then she turned to Violet and said, 'Call me. Every day.'

'She will,' he said, and, anxious to get her away, he supported her down the stairs, steering her through the wreckage of the hall until they reached the front door, not permitting her to stop, mourn.

'Don't look back,' he warned as she hesitated, momentarily dug in her heels. 'Always look ahead, keep your eyes on where you're going.'

'If only I knew where that was.'

She looked up at him, and then, because he wanted to reassure her, he bent and kissed her.

It had been an impulse. An attempt to distract her. Distract himself, maybe. But the softness of her lips, clinging to his, seemed to light a fire that had been smouldering within him since the moment he had first set eyes on her.

A recognition.

'Wherever it is,' he said, 'I will be with you. For as long as you need me.'

CHAPTER FIVE

VIOLET felt numb. As they sped towards the airport, enfolded in the luxurious leather of his car, the only warmth came from Sheikh Fayad's hand, holding hers as if he would never let it go.

Her hand. And her mouth.

She knew why he'd kissed her. He'd seen how hard it was to walk away from her home when they both knew that she'd never be going back. It had been no more than a distraction. He'd wanted to divert her, get her over the step, down the path, through the gate and into his car. To keep her from looking back.

And it had worked.

While her lips had clung to his, she'd had the feeling that there was nothing in the world that could hurt her. That there was no past, only a future. That with him she was safe.

She hoped it was true, because she'd put herself entirely in his hands. Good hands. Strong, gentle, she thought, looking at her own wrapped in his long fingers as he continued to hold on, never once letting go, despite the constant stream of calls he took on his cellphone.

Even when they arrived at the airport and a member of the VIP ground staff would have whisked her away, as if that were the norm, he just tightened his grip and said, 'Leave her. She stays with me.'

Only when they were in the air and he'd escorted her to an

unbelievably luxurious sitting room did he finally release her hand, delivering her into the care of the young woman waiting there.

'Rest now. Leila will be your companion. She will take care of you,' he said. 'No one will disturb you.'

Too late. She was disturbed beyond repair. But she managed a hoarse, 'Thank you.'

He responded with a frown. 'Why do you thank me? You have given me all you have while I have brought nothing but trouble to you and your friends.'

'I returned what is rightfully yours. As for the rest—you told Sarah that it was not her fault. Well, it's not yours, either.' Then, because he seemed lost for an answer, 'They will be safe?'

This morning she'd been so arrogant in her dismissal of danger. How could she have been so stupid? If anything happened to them…

'They will come to no harm, *insh'Allah*,' he said. 'By the will of God.' Then, with a smile, 'And the best security that money can buy.'

And then he was gone, leaving her to the pampering of Leila.

'Come. Bathe, sleep,' she said. 'You will feel better.'

She'd certainly look better. Forget her face. She'd thrown on the first things that had come to hand that morning when she'd dashed off to fetch Molly from playgroup. An old T-shirt on which she'd experimented with a design that not even her best friend would wear—let alone buy—and a pair of jeans that she'd bought in the market.

'So much for being a princess,' she said. 'I don't exactly look the part, do I?'

'I'm so sorry, *sitti*.' Leila was all flustered apology. 'I did not mean…'

Oh, good grief, the poor girl thought she was offended. 'I'm a mess, Leila. Honestly, you don't have to be polite.'

'Oh.' Then, indicating her suitcases, which had not been

placed in the hold but in the bedroom—this was travelling, but not as she knew it—'I'll find something for you to wear.'

Violet's first response was to explain that she was perfectly capable of looking through a suitcase, but she choked back the words as she realised that Leila would be hurt, feel rejected.

'Thank you.' Then, 'Maybe you can help me choose something that would make me look a little more…?'

'The part?' she offered, repeating the word with a tentative smile.

Which was what?

Sheikh Fayad called her Princess.

Never in a million years, she thought.

Presentable was about as much as she could hope for. Less of a wimpy embarrassment.

'"The part" will do nicely,' she said, managing a smile of her own, and leaving Leila, considerably happier, to sort through her clothes, while she wallowed in the luxury of the bathroom. Soaking the hideous night, the unbelievably worse day, out of her bones.

What was it Sarah had said about needing a little excitement in her life?

How about flying in a wide-bodied jet that would make anything in the Queen's Flight look like economy. Flying at thirty thousand feet, up to her neck in scented bubbles. Being flown away on a metaphorical magic carpet to some strange and exotic country by a man who would light up any woman's dreams.

She lifted wet fingers to her lips and smiled. A man whose chosen method of distracting a woman in distress was to kiss her. How much better could it get?

No. She definitely wasn't going there…

It had been no more than his way of preventing her from descending into hysteria, she knew. But for a moment, as his lips had claimed hers, held them for what had seemed like endless moments, it had felt like… She grinned. It had felt like skiing down Everest.

When she emerged from the bathroom, this time in a soft snowy white bathrobe, her hair wrapped in one of those fancy towels that soaked up the water, Leila was waiting, and had her hair dry and glossily straight in no time flat. Clearly she wasn't the standard cabin crew member; her duties extended well beyond providing peanuts and mineral water.

'You will rest now,' she said, turning back the bed. 'I will iron your clothes and repack them properly.'

'No…'

Leila frowned.

'No, really—I can't expect you to do that.'

'It is my pleasure,' she said, gathering up her bags and, leaving her with nothing but a pair of clean but crumpled cotton PJs, which she'd laid out as carefully as if they were made of silk, she headed for the door.

Fayad had to force himself to concentrate. Apart from the speculation that cutting short his visit to London was bound to provoke, stirring up more rumours about his grandfather's health, it meant a great deal of work for his staff as they cancelled meetings, lunches, receptions.

He made some calls himself, offering apologies for his abrupt change of plan, discussing alternative dates, leaving his diary secretary to confirm the details. But all the time, at the back of his mind, was Violet.

She had brushed aside the first attempt to steal the knife as if it had been nothing. But the wanton destruction of her home was an act of terrifying violence, rage, even, impossible to dismiss with the same casual courage. He understood why, instead of calling her closest friend, or even the police, she had called the only person she knew who would understand. Who wouldn't torment her with questions but would simply act.

It wasn't her safety that bothered him now. No one would harm her while she was in his care. But there was another problem.

In dropping everything and going to her aid he'd broken just about every protocol, crashed through every barrier that existed within his society between a man and a woman who was not his wife.

He could have done no less.

Seeing her, crumpled up like some broken, wounded creature, a man would have had to have had a heart of flint not to act as he had done, and everyone would understand that.

But there were consequences. It had not been a private matter. Too many of his staff had seen him holding her.

Everything else might have been accepted, even the kiss, but not that intimacy, and he had no doubt that his grandfather would hear of it long before he reached home. This would not be treated as some minor indiscretion to be overlooked; not when the consequences would suit the old man so well.

If she'd been anyone else it would not have mattered. As a foreign woman it would have been understood that she did not live by their rules. If she'd remained in London, even, it might have been possible to brush it aside.

But by taking her home, presenting her to his grandfather, he was giving her the status to which she was entitled, and as far as the court was concerned his marriage to Violet Hamilton would be a foregone conclusion.

To offer her anything less would be an insult to her and would certainly outrage the Sayyid family, happy to use whatever insult that came to hand in pursuit of discord. Even when it was an insult to the offspring of a daughter who had shamed them.

They'd gladly use it to manufacture a schism that they could use to drive the country apart and fuel their grab for control of the oil revenues that were—for the moment—pouring into the country.

The offer, with a dower fit for a princess, would have to be made, and in truth it was a marriage that would serve every imaginable purpose. From an aristocratic family, Violet was returning the symbol of their country's origins, redressing an old wrong with no thought of reward. Restoring her family's honour. Neutralising the Sayyid threat.

It was a marriage that would delight his grandfather and give Fayad a wife of great character, great beauty, while reuniting two great tribes who had for far too long been enemies beneath the diplomatic display of unity.

All attributes that made it a perfect match for him. Except one.

He dragged a hand over his face as if to wipe away the memories that haunted him. The loss of his wife, his son, had ripped the heart out of him and, despite all efforts to tempt him to offer for the treasure of one of the carefully nurtured daughters who would doubtless have made the perfect wife, he had been immune.

His family had been in danger and he had not been there to keep them safe. No man could live through that and be whole ever again…

Violet Hamilton was a chance to redeem himself, and in that first moment when he had set eyes on her, when she'd opened the door thinking it was just another day and looked up at him, any man would have responded to her as the desert to rain.

Even now he could feel the warmth of her body as he'd held her close, the softness of her breasts against his chest, the scent, the silk of her hair against his cheek.

Feel the soft tug of her lips against his…

'Sheikh?'

He looked up to see his aide regarding him anxiously and he shook his head, dismissing his concern with a gesture. Drank from the glass of water at his hand. It made no difference.

Violet woke to the steady thrumming of the aircraft's engines, for a minute completely disoriented. Then, as she rolled over, luxuriating in the feel of the finest linen sheets, it all came back with a rush.

The *khanjar.*

Her home.

Sheikh Fayad.

She was flying to Ras al Kawi in the kind of luxury that she could only ever have dreamed of. She concentrated on that rather than the horror she'd left behind.

'You are awake, *sitti*…' Leila placed a tray on the table beside the bed containing orange juice, fresh figs, small cakes. 'We will be landing in an hour,' she said, with a shy smile. 'Sheikh Fayad asked if he might be permitted to join you before we touch down?'

Be permitted? Then, as she sipped at the orange juice, her brain caught up. Obviously the meaning had become distorted in translation.

'I imagine he wants to drill me in the rules of court etiquette,' she said, putting two and two together and coming up with a little inventive translation of her own. 'Teach me when to curtsey and remind me that princesses only speak when they're spoken to.' And who could blame him?

Leila looked shocked. 'No! That would be most…'

'What?'

'Everything will be very different for you in Ras al Kawi, I think.'

'No doubt,' she said, swinging her legs to the floor. 'But even a girl from the wrong side of Camden Market knows that rule number one is never keep a sheikh waiting.'

Leila giggled. 'A woman must always keep a man waiting.'

'Really?'

'Until he has…' She sought for a word. 'Overwhelmed her and he is her lord.' And she blushed, leaving what she meant by "overwhelmed" crystal-clear.

'Okaaay,' Violet said, lost for any other response. 'I'll, um, just freshen up, and then you can help me pick out something suitable to wear.'

That brought a smile to the girl's face. 'I have already chosen,' she said.

'Oh, right.' Well, she'd had plenty to choose from. It was

obvious that whoever had packed had emptied her wardrobes. Brought everything.

Left to her own devices, she'd have chosen her denim ankle-length skirt and a fine knitted top that covered her arms. Maximum skin coverage. She knew better than to offend Fayad's grandfather with some flighty western garment. A bare midriff. Too much leg.

But apparently that didn't come close to what Leila considered appropriate. Given the run of Violet's wardrobe, she'd picked out one of her student design pieces. A richly decorated evening outfit that she'd made for an end-of-term college fashion show.

'This is very beautiful,' Leila said. 'It will be perfect for your arrival in Ras al Kawi.'

"This" was a long skirt in a curious shot silk that in one light was blue-grey, in another a soft turquoise, that the stallholder—and he was a smooth-tongued man if ever there was one—had sworn matched her eyes exactly.

The fabric had been way beyond her budget, but, totally unable to resist something so gorgeous, she'd traded half a dozen of her precious one-off embroidered T-shirts, made for the co-operative stall she'd set up with some of her college mates.

She'd appliquéd the skirt with a fan of velvet and silk peacock "eyes", free-hand embroidered the fine feathers using her sewing machine.

She hadn't had enough material to make a jacket, but had instead made a neat little waistcoat which, for the fashion show, she'd worn with one invisible hook at the breast and nothing else. It had been a huge success with the audience, if not with the *avant garde* college lecturers, who'd pronounced it too "conservative". Too "wearable". But then that was all she'd ever wanted to design and make—clothes that women longed to wear.

But a few days later she'd come home from a meeting of the

co-op, full of their plans to expand, set up a proper business, to find her grandmother collapsed with the first of her strokes.

Three years on from college, her outfit, like her plans, her first step on the way to her own fashion label, seemed like a fantasy. Rich, gorgeous, but not the sort of thing you'd actually wear except to a pretty fancy party. Even with the co-ordinating top that she'd made to wear beneath the waistcoat.

Struggling to bite back the *I don't think so* which flew to her lips, she said, 'It seems rather exotic, Leila. Do you really think it would do?'

'Oh, yes,' she said, with absolute confidence. 'It is quite perfect.'

In that case she was in trouble, she thought as Leila produced the hair straighteners to tidy up the curls that had made a bid for freedom while she slept. Then tutted as she insisted on applying the minimum of make-up herself.

'You need kohl to emphasise your eyes and your hands should be hennaed,' she insisted, and maybe she was right—about the kohl at least. She looked washed-out, and without a little colour the clothes would be wearing her rather than the other way around.

There was no time to draw elaborate patterns on her hands with henna, but she allowed Leila to add kohl and a touch of blusher, although Violet wiped off most of the kohl as soon as she'd turned away to pick up her skirt, hooking, buttoning and zipping her up, as if she hadn't been doing it herself for her entire life.

The waistcoat followed, and when Violet looked at the finished result in the mirror she swallowed. This was as good as her wardrobe got. Her Cinderella "you *can* go to the ball" outfit; if this was what constituted everyday wear in Ras al Kawi, what on earth did women wear when they wanted to make an impression?

What would make an impression on Sheikh Fayad?

She stopped the thought and turned to face Leila. 'What do you think?' she asked. 'Will I do?'

Leila's response was a sigh of envy. 'It is designer?' she asked, and Violet's smile was, finally, unforced.

'In a manner of speaking,' she said. Then, when the girl frowned, 'I designed it, Leila. And then I made it.' Since the girl was apparently lost for words, she said, 'Have we kept Sheikh Fayad waiting long enough, do you think?'

CHAPTER SIX

FAYAD looked up as his aide approached him. 'The Princess is waiting,' he said.

He'd given no instructions that she was to be given that title, but everyone knew who she was, and it seemed that her transformation from Violet Hamilton to Princess Violet al Sayyid had already begun.

He still did not know what he was going to say to her, only that he must somehow prepare her for his grandfather's expectations. Reassure her that she was totally in control of her own destiny. But as the door to the *hareem majlis* was opened to his knock he saw her standing in the centre of the room, waiting for him, and words became an irrelevance.

He could not have spoken even if he'd wanted to.

Grave, beautiful, untouchable.

As distant from the girl who'd opened the door to him that morning—hair an enticingly damp tangle of curls, legs and feet bare, wearing nothing but a faded pink bathrobe—as the moon was from the stars.

Mistaking his silence for disapproval, she said, 'This was Leila's idea.' A tiny gesture took in her clothes, some rich creation that would have his sisters drooling with envy.

'Leila will be rewarded,' he said.

'Oh. I wasn't sure. I thought it seemed a little…excessive, but…'

'But everything is strange.'

Her silence, her stillness were answer enough.

'You are wondering, now you've had time to think, whether you have made a mistake.' And this time heat rushed to her cheeks. Not that cool, then.

'You have the *khanjar*,' she said. 'And now you have me. If this was a movie I would probably be screaming at the heroine not to be so dumb.'

'Believe me, I appreciate the trust you have shown. Your generosity. You could so easily have told me to…how do you say it? Get lost? Sold the *khanjar* to the highest bidder.'

She could have no idea how high the bidding would have gone.

'No. That would have been wrong. And I'm here to protect Sarah. Her family. The innocent people who get hurt when powerful people clash.'

'Not even a little bit for yourself? Are you not curious about your family? About where you come from?'

'I could have gone to the library,' she said, continuing to regard him with those extraordinary eyes. Then, 'Your only concern was to get me away from the house. Anyone else would have called the police, but you didn't want them involved, did you?'

'My country's politics are not the concern of your police, Princess.'

'Don't call me that. I'm not a princess. I'm just Violet Hamilton.'

'And you're angry with me. You find yourself being torn from everything you know and you're just a little frightened.'

'Of course I'm frightened!' she said. 'It's been a hell of a day…'

Without thinking, he reached out and took her hand in what he'd intended as no more than a gesture of simple reassurance, but he continued to hold it long after it became much more.

Beneath his, her hand was small, but not soft. There was nothing soft about her. He had her history and he knew she had given up her education to care for her grandmother, not for expectation of reward, but out of love.

She was a woman whose value was far above rubies. Far beyond him…

'Are you afraid now? Truly?'

'Should I be?'

'What does your heart tell you?'

Violet shook her head. The nonsense that her heart was babbling as he held her hand, warmed her with the heat of his eyes, was for her ears alone.

In a suit, Sheikh Fayad had been drop-dead gorgeous. Attainable, if only in some foolish midnight fantasy. But here, in snowy robes, a silver *khanjar* at his waist, he was a figure from another world. One that was so far beyond anything she knew that she could see just how foolish any fantasy involving him would be.

'My heart says that it's a bit late for second thoughts,' she replied, retrieving her hand.

The fact was, she'd rushed into this without a clue about where she was going, or what to expect.

'It is only natural to feel anxious, but I promise you will be made most welcome.'

'Even though Princess Fatima stole the *khanjar* from you?' she asked.

'That worries you? It need not. You will be honoured for returning it.' Then, 'Shall we sit down? I will do my best to answer any questions. Explain what will happen when we arrive at Ras al Kawi.'

He indicated one of the armchairs, waited while she settled herself before taking the one beside her.

Questions. Dozens of questions had been racing through her mind, but mostly about where she would stay.

One thing was sure. She could not expect the undivided attention of the heir to the throne so, while she had it, she'd better make the most of it.

'Tell me about Ras al Kawi?' she asked.

It was the right question, his smile transforming his grave countenance into something very different. Making him seem younger, less…haunted. Sarah, she realised, had been quite wrong when she'd warned her about some man charming her out of her windfall.

If he'd smiled she would have been on her guard, suspected his motives. Wouldn't have been so quick to hand over the *khanjar.* So quick to pick up the phone and call him.

That quiet, austere gravity was far more deadly.

'What is it like?' she pressed.

'A great traveller once said that Ras al Kawi sits like a dragon's tooth between Ramal Hamrah and Ras al Hajar,' he told her, 'but within the fortress of the mountains our valleys are fertile and green, and the coast brings us fish and pearls.'

'There is no desert?'

'You British are all the same. What is this yearning you have for empty spaces where the wind continually removes any trace of man? Great shifting dunes?' He shook his head, but his smile intensified as if it pleased him to tease her a little.

Encouraged, she grinned, said, 'Blame Omar Sharif in *Lawrence of Arabia.*'

'Not the fabled Lawrence himself?'

'He was a little…intense.'

'Indeed,' he said, his brows twitching slightly at her choice of word. 'And we do have desert. Beyond the mountains. Flat, arid scrub with an endless horizon. And beneath it the oil and gas field that gives our country its wealth.'

'You have everything, then.'

'Ras al Kawi is a country that many have coveted. It is strategically placed to command the sea, and through the centuries invaders have left their mark on the landscape, on the people. Your eyes, Princess, are the legacy of some Portuguese pirate, or maybe a Caucasian soldier who came this way with Alexander, leaving his seed before returning home.'

His passion for his home was genuine enough. He would, she thought, do anything to keep it from harm.

'No matter how beautiful a place is, in the end people always choose home,' she said.

'I hope so.'

It was impossible to miss the meaning in his words, that Ras al Kawi was her home, too, but she was generations away from his world.

As she'd dressed she'd had time to think about what she'd done. She knew she'd been rushed into a decision when she was afraid, not so much for herself as for the people around her, friends and neighbours who'd been a tower of strength in the last months, when leaving her grandmother, even for an hour, had felt like a betrayal.

She would never forget the image of the man with his arm about Sarah's throat, and yet the idea that the theft was politically motivated seemed, at a safe distance, to be unlikely. She'd just been targeted by local villains who'd read about her discovery in the local paper and thought she'd be easy prey.

She looked across at her hero. The man who'd raced to her side the moment she'd called. She might not have been swept off her feet by a desert warrior thundering across the sand on his stallion, but on reflection the black limousine was a fair approximation—bearing in mind that London was a tad short on the sand front—as was the private jet flying her thousands of miles from home to a very foreign country.

He hadn't been kidding about her being treated like a princess, though.

'When we arrive, there will be a formal reception party waiting for me,' he said, breaking into her thoughts. 'You will be driven straight to the palace. Leila will be with you,' he assured her.

'Am I about to be whisked off to your harem?' she asked, only half joking. It had been a very odd day.

'Of course,' he replied. 'You'll join a thousand women wearing nothing but filmy veils and jewels in their navels, each desperately hoping that tonight they'll be the one summoned to my bed.'

For a moment she couldn't breathe. Then she said, 'You're kidding, right?'

'I'm kidding,' he agreed. 'But not about the harem, although the word is *hareem*.' He gestured around them. 'And you are already part of it.'

'I am?' She swallowed nervously.

'The word simply means women. *Al hareem* means no more than the women of the house.' Then he shrugged. 'If it helps, I can assure you that no man in my family has had more than one wife in nearly a century.' Then, with a shrug, 'Apart from my father, who has had seven. But only one at a time. Even so my grandfather disinherited him, and he sulks in self-imposed exile in Europe.'

'Do you miss him?'

'He was never there to be missed, Princess.'

'Something we have in common, then. My father rarely slept in his own bed, either.'

'And your mother? Did she leave him?'

'In a manner of speaking. She took an overdose. I don't suppose she meant to kill herself, just shake him up, but there was a traffic hold-up, and my father was late home, by which time it was too late to save her.' At least that was the story she'd been told. 'Or maybe he just didn't bother to call anyone until it was too late. A man who would blackmail his mother, demand money in return for the surrender of his little girl, might do anything, don't you think?'

'That is what your grandmother used the money for? The equity release?'

'Twenty thousand pounds. She was too old to raise a mortgage, could not have made the repayments even if she had. Instead she borrowed against her only asset. I found his letter years ago.'

'I am sorry.'

She shook her head. 'You have brothers? Sisters?'

'My mother remarried. I have a brother, three sisters. Many nephews and nieces. They will all visit. Everyone will want to meet you.' Then, 'I should tell you that my wife and son were killed by a car bomb in Beirut. Hasna wanted to visit an aunt who lives there. I was too busy to go with them. They were not targets, just in the wrong place at the wrong time.'

And it was her turn to reach out, wordlessly lay her hand over his.

'No one will talk about it, and I did not want you to think there is a mystery,' he said, but there was an underlying hesitation in his demeanour, suggesting that he had something on his mind. Something that he was finding difficult to broach. 'It is only to save my feelings that they keep silent.'

'You should talk about them,' she said. 'Remember the things that brought you joy.'

He shook his head, but there was something bothering him. He certainly hadn't asked to see her to discuss the correct depth of curtsey when she met the Emir.

'What is it, Sheikh Fayad? What is it that you wanted to tell me?'

He lifted a brow. 'You are perceptive as well as astute, Princess.'

'It comes packaged as standard with the X chromosomes,' she replied. 'What's up? Are you trying to find some way to tell me that I'm going to have to wear a veil when I meet your grandfather?'

'Would you do that?' he asked.

She shrugged. 'I do understand that different societies have different expectations, and while I wouldn't be prepared to wear one on a regular basis, I wouldn't want to do anything to offend him.'

He shook his head, but he was smiling. 'There's no need for a veil. They are worn by women only on desert journeys, as protection against sun and sand, and the *abaya*, the cloak that covers head and clothes, is worn as protection against dust and heat.'

'How do they live? What are their lives like?' she asked.

'Those who are educated and wish to work are employed in medicine, business, teaching. Nothing is *haram*. Forbidden.'

'What about those who are not educated? Isn't schooling compulsory?'

'Not for girls. And there are few jobs for the uneducated. They are forced to stay at home, work in the home, on the land.'

'Captive labour?'

'That is, perhaps, a little harsh. They do what women have been doing for centuries. It is, however, my intention to change that when I become Emir. We need all our people to be educated so that they can play their part in building our country.'

He regarded her thoughtfully for a moment, his fine dark eyes searching her face as if weighing his words. She'd felt the silk of his skin against her temple as he'd held her. Wanted to reach out now and run her fingers over his cheeks, above his lip, feel his mouth against hers…

'I wish it were something as trivial as whether or not you should wear a veil,' he said, turning abruptly away.

'Now I'm really worried.'

'No…' He shook his head. 'Trust me, Violet. Whatever happens you need have no fears for yourself. I am the one who has been…' He lifted his hand in a gesture that in anyone else she might have described as helpless. There was nothing helpless about Sheikh Fayad. '…thoughtless. Reckless with your reputation.'

'My reputation?'

She would have laughed. This was the twenty-first century, and girls didn't have "reputations" any more. At least not in her world. But obviously for him this was no laughing matter, and so she kept her mouth in order.

'In my society to be alone with a woman, to hold her as I held you—'

'You were comforting me,' she said, doing her best to reassure him that he had done nothing to offend her, although she suspected that somehow it went beyond that. 'I was falling apart and you held me together.'

'I did a great deal more than that, Princess.' And he turned to face her. 'Much more.'

The kiss...

'Only because you thought I was going to have hysterics at leaving my home. It was nothing,' she said quickly, but could not meet his eyes.

It had not felt like "nothing". It had felt like a bridge between the past and the future. And how easily she had stepped towards the unknown, leaving everything, everyone she knew, behind her. Because with his lips on hers she had not cared if she ever came back.

'And who would know?' she said.

'Staff from my embassy, those who were at your house, who packed your clothes, stayed to organise the clean-up. And because they know it is inevitable that my grandfather will have heard exactly what happened today and drawn his own conclusions.' Then, 'And *I* know.'

CHAPTER SEVEN

FAYAD's words were spoken with a finality that raised Violet's heartbeat.

'What conclusions? What are you saying?'

'My world is not like yours, Princess. Here marriages are arranged. It is a contract that unites families, matches two people who might never have met except perhaps as children. Whose qualities are known only by word of mouth. Through friends, family.'

'What about those career women? You can't work without meeting people.'

'There are not so many. Many families still cling to old traditions. Your own family, for instance, the Sayyid,' he said, with an impatient gesture, 'they fight change with every breath.'

It was something he clearly felt very strongly about.

'Sometimes you have to bite the bullet, break eggs, to get things done,' she said.

'The problem with that, Princess, is that sometimes more than the eggs will break.'

'I'm sorry. I'm a little out of my league here.' Then, because she couldn't keep her mouth shut, 'Can you really trust the word of people who for politics, money, might have a vested interest in arranging a wedding?'

'Believe me, when a wedding is being arranged everyone has an opinion and everyone expresses it. Everything that you ever did will be dragged out and examined at length by grandmothers, sisters, cousins, brothers, aunts.' He smiled again. 'Especially aunts…' Then, 'It is too important to risk failure. Marriage is the glue of a civilised society and everyone has a stake in its success.' He watched her struggle with that, then, before she could ask the next question, he said, 'Yes, Violet. A girl can reject any potential groom.'

'But they do meet before the wedding? These couples?'

'Maybe. Not always. And not once the wedding preparations begin.' He smiled at her disbelief. 'A bride is a treasure to be closely guarded within the family while the dower is gathered and delivered. In that period she will only see those closest to her. Even when the contracts have been signed and the bride and groom are to all intents and purposes married.'

'What happens then?'

'Between the formal signing and the celebrations? First the engagement jewels are sent. Not just a ring, but a matching set of bracelets, necklace, earrings, in stones chosen by the groom's mother to perfectly complement his bride. At the same time the groom prepares a house for her, furnishing it with the best he can afford. And the dowry is gathered—gold, jewellery, bolts of every kind of cloth, carpets, money, all designed to demonstrate his ability to provide for her—ready to be delivered to the bride's home to be displayed at the *maksar*, the formal gathering of women to celebrate the marriage. Although the bride herself will not take part in that.'

'Oh…'

Violet, who had been thinking it all sounded rather cold, began to see it from a different point of view. Began to imagine the trembling excitement of a secluded virgin bride as the day grew nearer. As her groom's dowry gifts arrived, proving to the world, to her family, to her, just how much he valued her, wanted her above all other women.

'There is more than one way to rouse the passions,' she said.

'Her weight in gold?'

Her eyes widened at the idea of just how much that would

be worth, but then she shook her head. 'No. It's not the gold. It's what it represents,' she said. And Sheikh Fayad responded with a look of admiration for her understanding. A look that sent her own heart spinning up into her mouth, that suggested passion would not be in short supply for the woman who won his heart.

Drawn in, totally fascinated, she said, 'Tell me about the wedding.'

'When everything is ready, there will be a vast celebration. In the old days tribes would come in from the desert and set up camp. The feasting will go on for weeks, until finally the time comes for the groom to demand entrance to the bride's home, to fight his way through her family to claim his bride, who will be waiting, wrapped in layer upon layer of veils, sitting on a white sheet.'

Even as he described the scene her heart rate was spiralling out of control, and she only managed to hold back the exclamation that sprang to her lips by holding her hand over her mouth. Cold? No way…

'Is something wrong?' Sheikh Fayad asked.

'No,' she managed, resisting the urge to fan her cheeks at the thought of him removing layer after layer of veils, unwrapping her… 'I'm fine. Really,' she said, when he reached forward, poured her a glass of iced water that seemed to evaporate on her tongue. 'You did this? When you married?'

He didn't immediately answer and she back-pedalled madly. 'Oh, Lord, please forget I asked that. I can't believe I was so rude. I didn't mean—'

'The bride is expected to fight, too. To bite and kick, protect her virtue with all her strength so that her husband will respect her.'

'And does he?'

Had Hasna fought? she wondered. Could she have looked at this beautiful man and not fallen instantly and whole-heartedly in love with him? Could any woman?

And if, because his respect would be something unbelievably

precious, she'd fought him with ever fibre of her being, how had he overwhelmed her?

Even as the question welled up in her mind, she knew the answer. She'd lashed out at him this morning—angry, hurting—and he'd sat with her on her grandmother's bed, just holding her, taking the blows, whispering soft words of comfort, his lips against her hair, her temple, gentling her, calming her. In her head she saw how that scene might eventually unfold with his bride. There would be no force, but patience, a soft voice, quiet kisses, caresses that would open her to him as a flower opened to the light and warmth of the sun.

And she understood exactly what he'd meant when he'd said that he'd done "much more". It wasn't the fact that he'd kissed her. His kiss had been the least of it…

She swallowed, took another sip of water. In a desperate attempt to blot out what was happening in her head, she said, 'Having showered her with jewels, and fought her entire family, the groom then has to overcome his bride, too? He doesn't exactly get it easy, does he?'

Making light of it.

He smiled. 'Interesting. I had assumed your sympathies would be with the bride.'

'Oh, please,' she said quickly. 'It doesn't take a psychologist to work out that this is a well-thought-out strategy to overcome those initial awkward moments.' Then, 'I imagine any bride worth her weight in gold knows exactly the right moment to go all weak and swoony.'

To surrender to her groom's strength, his power, and in doing so claim it for her own.

Just as she had done. Fighting him, furious with him. Blaming him for what had happened one moment. Surrendering to the comfort he offered the next.

'Three generations has done nothing to dilute your understanding, Princess,' Sheikh Fayad said, apparently not making the connection—which should have been a relief but, oddly, was not—and merely amused at her perception. 'You are Arab to the bone.'

'It's just common sense,' she said, not in the least bit amused.

'Maybe,' he said, eyes suddenly thoughtful. 'So? Would you consider such an arrangement?'

'Me? Who's going to seek *me* out for an arranged marriage? What do *I* have to offer?' Then, as it clicked, as she realised what all that stuff about his grandfather, what all this had been leading up to, she said, 'Oh, no! No way!' And holding up a hand as if to fend him off, 'That's ridiculous. Really.'

So why, inside her head, was her subconscious saying, *Oh, yes! How soon? Really!*

'I assure you, Princess, that a marriage between us would make my grandfather the happiest man in the world. It has been his dearest wish that I remarry—he refuses to retire until I do. And you have every quality to recommend you.'

'I don't think so.'

'There is no need for concern, Princess. I was simply explaining why I will have to make an offer. Putting you on your guard against the expectations of my family.'

Oh, right. Well, that was plain enough. He would make the offer because he had no choice. And since, obviously, marriage was the furthest thing from his mind, her role was to get him off the hook and say no.

As if she'd say anything else. They'd only met that morning, for heaven's sake!

So why did she suddenly feel rejected, unwanted, just a little bit…hollow?

'I understand, Sheikh Fayad,' she said.

And she did. No matter that her great-great-grandmother had been Princess Fatima al Sayyid. They came from different worlds and this would never be hers. No matter that they'd already spent more time together than the average Ras al Kawi couple before they got down to business on the white sheet.

'Thank you for taking the time to explain it all so clearly. You need have no concerns.'

He frowned, looked as if he might say something more, but there was a ping, and the seatbelt lights came on, and instead he said, 'We are about to land.'

This time he did not sit with her, hold her hand. Instead Leila came to escort her to a small cabin at the rear of the plane, while he joined his staff in the forward cabin.

She told herself that she did not mind. She'd had the extraordinary privilege of spending time alone with the Sheikh and she would always cherish that. But now they were in Ras al Kawi things would be different.

How different she realised as soon as they'd landed, and she and Leila were left to cool their heels while a carpet was rolled up to the steps.

Sheikh Fayad and his party descended and approached the line of dignitaries waiting to greet him. Only then were Violet and Leila escorted down a separate set of steps that had been brought to the rear exit, where a limousine with tinted windows was waiting. Violet paused a few steps from the ground to take one last look across the tarmac at Sheikh Fayad who, every inch the Prince, was being greeted by the dignitaries. And she felt the strangest sensation of loss.

In London, on the aircraft, they could talk freely. Here, she realised, he was a man set apart. Out of reach.

As she hesitated, one of the men waiting to greet him turned and stared across the tarmac at her. His look was assessing, insolent, a little pleased, even, and for a moment she wished she had been wearing something anonymous, been draped head to foot in one of those black cloaks—an *abaya*—her face covered in a veil. She was glad that the car windows were tinted, so that as they sped away—no passport or immigration control for members of the Sheikh's party, obviously—she was… secluded.

* * *

Fayad faced his grandfather. Anger warred with the respect he owed him. Respect, marginally, won it. 'You cannot do this. The Princess is here as my guest…'

'She is their kin, Fayad. Their daughter. Ahmed al Sayyid is here, waiting to take her to their compound as soon as she has formally returned the Blood of Tariq.'

It was outrageous. 'Her home has been attacked twice already in an attempt to steal the *khanjar*, and I have no doubt that the Sayyid were behind that.'

'Fayad, please…'

His grandfather raised a hand. With a pang of remorse, he saw that it was shaking. In the short time that he'd been away the old man had deteriorated.

He reached out, took his grandfather's hand, held it.

'The responsibilities of a ruler are to his country, my son, not to an individual. The Sayyid will invoke tradition, and you know they will have support.'

'They have a medieval attitude to women. Their wives are kept behind high walls, their daughters are not allowed to go to school…'

'That is their way. I cannot defy them in this.'

But Fayad could, and would when the time came.

'Violet is giving up something of great value and asking for nothing in return except my protection. And I will protect her. It is a matter of honour.'

'We both know that there is only one way you can do that. But I warn you, if they believe you are attached to this woman, their dowry demands will put her beyond price.'

'They will dare ask for the Blood of Tariq?' Even as he said it, he knew that was their aim. They had not managed to steal the *khanjar*, but their spies would have informed them of every move he'd made in London. What had happened between him and Violet. Their outrage at their kinswoman's ruined honour would know no bounds. They did not care about her, but they would demand marriage, knowing that he could not refuse. And they would demand the Blood of Tariq as dowry.

His grandfather sighed. 'I'm sorry, Fayad. My hands are tied. Since they demand it, I have no choice but to surrender her to her family.'

He understood. He might rail against it, but to undermine the claim of family would be to deny the law, and his assurance, so confidently asserted, that a bride was free to choose now rang hollow in his ears.

Neither of them would have a choice.

To refuse the Sayyid terms would leave her a virtual prisoner in their compound. Beyond his reach.

He could not, would not, allow that to happen—even for a day.

There was no time to wonder, to marvel at the beauty of the palace, the exquisite arches, decorative tiling. No time to wonder at its size, spreading across the broad hilltop.

Below them lay the city, where wind towers, domes, delicate minarets sprawled down to a wide sweeping bay. Leila had pointed out landmarks.

The recently completed air-conditioned shopping mall. A new hotel with a glass atrium. The gold *souk*…

'What is that?' Violet had asked, as they'd climbed higher and she'd seen the remains of a cliff-top fortress.

'That?' Leila had shrugged. 'It's the Portuguese tower. It's just a ruin. There's nothing there,' she'd said, dismissing history with a careless gesture.

'It's all so much greener than I expected.'

'We have many parks. There—that is the *souk*. The market…' Parks were clearly not Leila's idea of a good time, either.

And then they'd driven through gates set in a high wall, guarded by armed men, and "green" had taken on an entirely new meaning.

Unlike European palaces, it was not one huge building but a series of small arched and domed buildings, grouped around colonnaded courtyards, each with a garden, trees. Formal pools were connected by a narrow continuous rill. Everywhere was shaded, scented by roses, jasmine, flowering shrubs that she had never seen before.

As they stepped from the air-conditioned car, the warmth, the intensity of the evening scents, wrapped themselves about her, and she felt like a flower opening to the sun. She turned slowly, taking in the exquisite tiled arches, the clear sky, now turning a darker blue as the sun sank behind distant mountains.

'It's so beautiful,' she said, but as she took a step towards the pool Leila restrained her.

'There's no time. You have to get ready to meet the Emir.'

They walked up marble steps into a vestibule spread with fine carpets. Leila kicked off her shoes and nodded approvingly when Violet followed her example.

'This is to be your house,' she said, hurrying her through a series of ornate reception rooms until they reached a private suite of sitting room, bedroom, bathroom. 'Make yourself comfortable, then I will prepare you for the Emir's *majlis*.'

'Majlis?'

'It is where he sits so that people can come and talk to him. Drink coffee. Appeal for his help. All the tribal leaders and heads of important families will be there today, to see the Blood of Tariq.'

Violet felt a sudden qualm. A surge of something rather more heavy-footed than butterflies stampeding through her stomach. A nervousness that was not eased when, having persisted in her determination to apply more make-up, Leila lifted a loose outer robe over her head and let it drop to the floor over her clothes.

It was cut from dark blue silk, embroidered in gold thread at hem and wrist, slit at the side. Ornate. Simple.

'This is a *thaub.* A traditional outer garment.'

'It's exquisite.'

'You will wear a scarf?' Without waiting for an answer, Leila loosely draped a long matching scarf over her head. It was woven from a silk so fine that it appeared to defy gravity, almost to float as the air was stirred by a slowly turning ceiling fan.

'Beautiful,' Leila said.

'It's lovely,' Violet agreed. She knew cloth, and understood that this was something rare, beyond anything she could ever afford.

'Not the scarf. You, Princess.' She fiddled with the tail of a comb until Violet's face was framed in a dark curve of hair. 'You are beautiful.'

'No…'

Unusual. Dramatic. That was the kindest thing anyone had ever said about her looks. Even her grandmother.

Her nose was too big, her brows too strong, and her eyes were the wrong colour… And yet made up this way, her hair shining like polished ebony, her face gently framed in the soft folds of the scarf, it seemed as if suddenly everything had fallen into place. Everything…fitted.

'Good. Hurry. The car is waiting…'

CHAPTER EIGHT

FAYAD paced the small lobby, waiting for Violet to arrive. There would be so little time to explain. Then, as the door opened, he turned and caught his breath, felt his heart seize at the sight of her.

Again.

She kicked off her shoes as naturally as if she'd been doing it all her life, stepped inside and stood, her head on one side, waiting for him to speak.

Speech was not enough. He touched his fingers to his forehead, his heart, bowed to her beauty, her honour, her courage. 'You are, in every sense of the word, a princess, Violet Hamilton.' Then, 'Give me your hands.'

She held them out and he picked up the Blood of Tariq and placed it across her palms, held his own hands beneath them.

'By this act, Princess, you honour your family. They should be proud to call you daughter.'

'Should? That suggests they might *not* be best pleased that I'm surrendering this to you.'

He did not want to frighten her with the truth, but since she was not a fool he tilted his head, acknowledging that she might have a point.

'Will I meet them? Will they be here?'

'Ahmed al Sayyid, patriarch of his tribe—your tribe—is sitting at my grandfather's right hand.' And given the slightest opportunity, he thought, would seize the chance to move over and drag his country back into the Dark Ages. His sons would be there, too. And if he failed to surrender the Blood of Tariq, she would be doubtless given to one of those cousins as a wife. Without the option to say no… 'He will expect you to bow to him, acknowledge him.'

'But I shouldn't expect a hug and a *Hi, kid, welcome home…*?'

'I'm afraid not.' Then, because time was short, 'My grandfather is sitting at the far end of the *majlis.* You should walk straight down the room, looking neither to left nor right, holding out the *khanjar* so that everyone can see it. Bow to Ahmed first. Then bow to my grandfather and place the knife in his hands. I will be with you every step of the way,' he said, and the tension seemed to slip away from her a little. Then, 'Do you remember what I promised you, Princess?'

She looked up at him. 'I remember,' she said. Then, fear darkening her eyes, 'Something has happened. What is it?'

'There's no time to explain. Do you trust me to do exactly as I promised, Princess?'

Violet looked up at him, her extraordinary eyes searching his as if looking for something. Whatever it was, she must have found it, because she said, 'I am here. I have flown thousands of miles, placed myself entirely in your hands, because you assured me that you would protect my friends.'

'And you, Princess. Protect you.' With every breath in his body. And he would, no matter what the cost. Honour—more—demanded it. 'After my grandfather thanks you in both Arabic and English, I will speak. When I turn to you I will ask you a question, you will answer *nam.* No matter what happens, you must do that. Do you understand?'

'Nam,' she repeated. 'What does it mean?'

'Yes.'

'I see. Am I allowed to ask what the question is?'

To his intense relief, the huge carved doors to the *majlis* swung open, making further explanations impossible.

'Three times,' he said urgently. 'I will ask and you will

answer.' Letting go of her hands, he stepped back, then, as she moved forward, he took his place at her side.

Fayad walked beside Violet towards his grandfather, his heart pounding. On either side of them he was aware of a stirring as the tribal leaders, elders, people's representatives rose to honour the *khanjar.* Or was it Violet, the very image of a Sayyid, who sent audible shockwaves through the reception room?

She faltered only once, catching her toe on the edge of one of the carpets that were laid over each other, and he reached out to steady her.

Beneath her sleeve, despite her stately progress, she was trembling, and he did not let go, keeping his hand possessively on her elbow. Staring down Ahmed al Sayyid who, as leader of the second most powerful tribe of his nation, was indeed at his grandfather's right hand.

Violet stopped in front of the two men, bowed her head to acknowledge Ahmed, then, taking Fayad by surprise, instead of bowing to his grandfather, she knelt before him, extending the *khanjar,* and, eyes cast down, placed it into his hands, saying simply, 'In the name of Fatima al Sayyid I return the Blood of Tariq to its rightful place.'

Ahmed al Sayyid was scowling furiously at her, but his grandfather smiled.

'Thank you, child. Welcome home.'

Ahmed rose to his feet, but before he could speak Fayad, following Violet's dramatic example, joined her on his knees and, reaching for her hand, took it and declared, 'I call upon you all to witness that I take Violet Hamilton al Sayyid as my wife.' Then he turned to her and said, 'Do you accept me as your husband?'

Ahmed took a step towards him, but his grandfather raised a hand to stop him.

She looked at him for what seemed a lifetime, and then she said, *'Nam.'*

He repeated his statement and again said, 'Do you accept me as your husband?'

'Nam.'

And a third time.

'Nam…'

Around them the room erupted in uproar, but he scarcely noticed as Violet lifted one of her exquisite brows a millimetre, as if to ask, *What have I done?*

He responded by lifting her hand to his lips, and murmured, 'You have just accepted me as your husband.' Then, raising her to her feet, he could not fail to miss the barely concealed smile of satisfaction on his grandfather's face as he embraced him, embraced Violet, with the words, 'Welcome, daughter…' Then, 'Give me your hand, Fayad.'

He extended it, expecting the old man to take it, hold it, but instead he raised it, placed the *khanjar* into it, holding it there for a long moment before turning to the *majlis* with the words, 'Salute your new Emir.'

Then he let go, stepped back, leaving Fayad centre stage.

It was pure theatre, and it occurred to him that when it came to playing games his grandfather had a fifty year head start on him.

He had been desperate to see him with a new wife—had used the threat of Ahmed al Sayyid to manipulate him. And now it was done, and he'd got his own way, he would retire to the mountains to spend his remaining days tending his soul, leaving his rivals with no choice but to smile and embrace not only Fayad's marriage, but his new position as ruler of Ras al Kawi.

His only thought was for Violet, who, when she realised what he'd done, would believe he had used her.

For an hour they stood, side by side, while every member of the *majlis* came to embrace him, make their bow to Violet, touch the *khanjar.*

She kept up a smile throughout, never faltered. Only someone who'd seen the real thing would know that it was a mask. And heaven alone knew what she was thinking behind it.

Finally it was over and, his hand beneath her elbow, he was able to escort her through the line of clapping elders.

The moment the doors closed behind them the smile vanished and she turned on him. 'Wife?' she breathed.

'It was necessary—'

'So that you could have your crown? Why didn't you tell me?

'There was no time…'

'No time? What happened to weeks of showering me with dowry to prove how much you value me?' she demanded, sweeping his attempt at explanation aside. 'The gold, the jewellery, the cloth? Actually, just the cloth would have done. I'm a dress designer, and cloth is always welcome, but then you didn't know that, did you? You didn't ask about my ambitions, about my life. You only care about your own.'

He hadn't asked because he knew. He knew all her history. But somehow he didn't think this was the moment to tell her that.

'In a crisis,' he said quietly, calmly, 'when the situation demands it, a declaration before witnesses serves the purpose.'

'Does it count if the bride hasn't a clue what's going on?'

'If you'll just listen, I will explain,' he said, taking her hand, moving her towards the door. This was not the place to be overhead having an argument with his bride.

She dug in her heels.

'How? You get a country and I get a cut-price registrar and two witnesses job. Is that all I'm worth?'

'I will tell you what you're worth,' he said, looping an arm around her waist and picking her up, carrying her over the threshold, leaving her shoes, leaving his.

He was determined to make her listen, to explain that a divorce would be as simple as the wedding, that all he'd done was protect her. But not here, where anyone might hear.

'Whatever happened to my much-vaunted chance to say

no?' she demanded, kicking out in an attempt to free herself, furious, hammering on his shoulders, his back. 'I trusted you, but your words are worth nothing, Fayad al Kuwani. I gave you your *khanjar* and you used it to buy your country. Used *me* to buy the alliance of the Sayyid.'

'Will you just listen to me?' he thundered. Forget calm. Forget quiet reason…

'Oh, that's right. Shout. The male answer to everything.'

'Violet, this isn't helping—'

'It's helping me.' She lifted her head, looked down at him. 'So, Your Emiri Highness? What happens now? I'm supposed to go away and get swaddled in veils, is that it? Sit on the white sheet and wait for you to come and unwrap me?'

So intent was she on making her point that she'd forgotten to struggle and, with a nod to the driver, he bundled her into the back of a waiting limousine.

They were cut off from the world, even from the driver, who was hidden behind a darkened wall of glass, but Violet was not frightened.

She was furious.

She'd given Sheikh Fayad everything he wanted. Fallen for all that fake sincerity. Believed him.

And here she was with a man—a virtual stranger—who'd tricked her into marrying him. Sitting in his lap, his arm around her, his breath warm against her hair.

Fight. She'd fight…

'You'd better be wearing body armour!' she warned.

And without warning Fayad laughed. How dared he laugh at her? 'I've married a cat,' he said. 'I'd always heard that Sayyid women fight like tigers.'

'I'm not Sayyid. I'm a Hamilton…'

'No, you're not, Violet. You're mine. You'll always be mine…' And he kissed her. Not gently. Not to distract her from some painful moment. But like some desert lord who, having captured his prize, aroused by the chase, was determined on making her his.

And that he was aroused she was in no doubt.

But that was his problem, not hers.

Her problem was that as his kiss became deeper, the satin pleasure of his tongue giving rather than taking, it was not him she was fighting but her own body's shockingly urgent response.

Need…

Desire…

She felt hampered by far too many clothes. The long skirt, the *thaub*, were encumbrances, not just holding her down but keeping them apart. She wanted freedom to move, wanted to feel his hand, his hot mouth upon her skin, upon breasts tight with need. Wanted him to soothe the heavy, yearning ache between her thighs.

She wanted, she discovered with a jolt of understanding, to be blissfully and repeatedly…overwhelmed.

And then, as swiftly as it had begun, it was over. But although the car had come to a standstill he did not move. Did not speak.

Fayad closed his eyes, for a moment just drinking in the pleasure of Violet, warm against him. Feeling once more the power of desire surge through him for the first time since the death of his family.

To the outside world he had seemed to recover. Carry on. Work for his country, his people. But inside everything that he was as a man had died on that day.

And now Violet had responded to him.

Angry, of course. She had every right to be. But above her anger was desire, hot and potent…

But to take advantage of that was beneath him.

For a moment he had forgotten himself. Had said that she was his. But that was not so. On the contrary. While she would always own a part of him, he had not taken her as his wife to bind her to him, but so that she could be free.

'Your house in London is now in your name, Violet,' he said, returning to reality. 'It is being remade. When it is done you will have a home in which you can be comfortable.'

'No...' Then, 'I don't understand.'

'You gave me everything you had. It is little enough in return. When you go home, I hope you will not think too badly of me.'

'You are sending me away?'

Dear God, she made it sound as if he were doing her an unkindness. If she knew how hard it would be to let her go. To walk away now...

'Not yet. Your house will not be ready for several months. It needs rewiring. New plumbing. You have dry rot...'

'It's a wonder it's still standing...'

'It will be as new. Until then, for form's sake, you will stay here.'

'And do what?'

'I promise nothing is expected of a new bride except to keep her husband happy.'

'Which means?'

He turned to her. 'Her husband will be happy if she is happy. That is your only duty. To be happy.'

'I don't understand.'

She never would.

'And then you'll have a house with good friends near you. A divorce settlement.'

'Divorce!'

He managed a smile. 'Divorce, you will be pleased to learn, is as easily done as marriage. It will be as if it had never happened.'

'Apart from the fact that you're now Emir.'

'Apart from that,' he agreed. 'You will return home, go back to college, found your fashion house if that is your wish.'

Violet slid from his arms, from his lap, to the seat beside him. 'I see.'

He'd done it again. Stilled her protest with a kiss. And

where moments before all she'd felt was liquid heat, now there was ice.

'How soon?'

'Three months.'

She glared at him. 'And what am I supposed to do for three months? Since pleasing my husband will not exactly fill my days?'

He glanced at her as if he might just change his mind about that.

'Don't worry about it,' she said hurriedly. 'I'll think of something.'

'Good.' Then, 'Of course you could help me break a few eggs.'

'Over your head?'

'What I had in mind was more in the nature of metaphorical eggs. My first action as Emir will be to announce that schooling is to be compulsory for girls, and it would be fitting if, as wife of the Emir, you were to lift the first spade of soil to mark the foundation of the Violet al Sayyid School for Girls.'

'Not al Kuwani?'

'Our women do not change their names on marriage.'

'Handy. It means you can really rub Ahmed al Sayyid's nose in it.'

'In what?' he asked. Then shook his head. 'You might be less sympathetic if I tell you that he would have taken you to his compound tonight if I had not intervened.'

'He couldn't do that!' Then, when he didn't agree, 'Could he?'

'He is your kin. The head of your family. My grandfather could not have stopped him without causing dissension. I should have foreseen the possibility…' He closed his eyes, as if to shut out how close a call it had been. 'Marriage was your only means of escape.'

And his promise to protect her would have left him no option but to act as he did.

'He would have demanded the Blood of Tariq as dowry, wouldn't he?'

He nodded.

He didn't say whether he would have surrendered it, and she didn't ask. To lose it would have weakened him politically. Maybe lost him the throne. What was his word to one woman—the kin of his enemy—against that?

'He was staring at me at the airport when we arrived.' She shivered, and for a moment she thought he was going to reach out to her again.

Instead he turned abruptly away, and in doing so answered any question she cared to ask.

'I wish I'd never found the wretched thing. It would have saved a lot of trouble all round.'

'Maybe. But it worked out well enough in the end. My grandfather has what he wanted. He is happy.'

She waited for him to say that it suited him, too, but he didn't. Well, he'd already gone to great trouble to explain that it was the last thing he'd wanted.

The marriage part, anyway.

His kiss, his arousal, his "you are mine" was no more than a reaction to her resistance. She'd challenged his masculinity. He'd overcome her…

Her only mistake had been to succumb too quickly.

She'd had the power to get what she wanted and had let it slip through her fingers. Not nearly Arab enough…

'Your grandfather won't be happy when you divorce me,' she said, pushing him. Testing him.

'I don't believe he'll be with us long enough to be disappointed.'

Her pride melted. 'He's really that sick?'

'It was only what he perceived as my stubbornness in defying him that was keeping him alive.'

'Why would you defy him? It's not as if you had to go out and find your own bride…'

'I was not ready.'

Damn it, he was still grieving for his wife. His son. And now he was about to lose a beloved grandparent. She was close enough to her own loss to understand what his feelings must be, no matter how little he showed.

Then she frowned.

'But…'

But if his grandfather was only weeks from death, why would Fayad use her when the Emiri throne was so close?

She let slip a very unprincesslike word.

She'd got it all wrong.

Everything.

'This wasn't about becoming Emir, was it? You really did do it entirely for me?'

'I gave you my promise that I would protect you.' He climbed from the car, offered her his hand. 'Go in now. Leila will be waiting.'

Go… 'But won't she expect…?' She stopped, blushing with confusion.

'She will expect me to build you a house, make you a dowry. Three months between the wedding and the marriage is not long.' Then, seeing her confusion, 'Just because the wedding was unconventional, it does not mean that the marriage formalities will not be observed.'

He leaned forward, kissed her forehead.

'I will see you tomorrow.'

CHAPTER NINE

THREE months had seemed an impossibly long time, and yet they flew by. Leila, now officially installed as her lady-in-waiting, was with her always, teaching her Arabic, the ways of Ras al Kawi.

She'd met Fayad's family, and was now taken to their heart, included on parties at the beach, shopping trips with his sisters. From being a girl with a family of one, a woman on her own, she was suddenly part of a huge extended family.

She found herself presiding over her own *majlis*. Like the Emir, she was there for all women to visit, to talk with, to bring their problems to as they drank tiny cups of coffee in the traditional way. She listened to their concerns and in turn, through Leila, talked about the value of education for their daughters.

And when she was taken by his sisters to visit the important *hareems*, especially the Sayyid *hareem*, she took that message with her, and found not just the younger women receptive, but their mothers and grandmothers, too.

It was the one thing she could do for Fayad, because he'd been right when he'd said, 'You're mine. You'll always be mine…' and the time she spent—running out faster than sand in an hourglass—was increasingly precious.

She might not be his wife in anything but name, but he treated her in every way like his queen. He discussed his ideas with her, took her with him when he visited schools, encouraged her input in the areas of women's health, employment.

He took her into the highlands and the valleys, to visit farms, smallholdings, to see for herself the life that his people lived there. The life the women lived. She'd expected hardship, and there was, but there was always warmth, hospitality, a simple joy in a life well lived.

They trekked across the desert—Violet swathed in veils, making him laugh out loud as her camel took her by surprise when it rose back legs first, so that she had to cling on for dear life to prevent herself being thrown over the creature's nose.

Everything was new, exciting, and she knew deep in her heart that the only thing that would make life better would be if, at the end of day, Fayad stayed with her instead of leaving her at her door. If he were truly her husband.

But he was careful always to keep a distance between them.

They were never alone. There were no more kisses. He did not reach for her hand.

Only sometimes she would turn and catch him looking at her, and for a moment she would believe that he felt the same way and her heart would turn over. But then he would look away and she'd know she was fooling herself.

She designed clothes for Leila, for Fayad's sisters, for her Sayyid cousins, and had them made up by a co-operative she'd set up for young girls who had no family. The workmanship was exquisite, and soon local women flocked to buy her designs, too, eager no doubt to please their new Emir. In her new position she discovered that there were no places barred to her, and she had a buyer from one of the big London stores coming to discuss an outlet for her label.

Breaking eggs.

There were rumblings of discontent about compulsory schooling for girls, she knew, stirred up by Ahmed al Sayyid, but they were muted, and when she visited the *souk* women reached out to touch her, whisper blessings.

And all the time her dowry accumulated at an alarming rate.

Each morning brought some new treasure. Diamonds in

every imaginable colour. One set, in a shade not quite blue, not quite green, Leila swore were a perfect match for her eyes. There were emeralds, sapphires, pearls. And gold. Mountains of the stuff. Bracelets, unbelievable necklaces that looked just like those she'd once seen in a photograph that were supposed to have been worn by Helen of Troy.

And then there were the rubies. Polished cabochon heart-red rubies. A stunning stone in a simple gold setting. A tumble of them in a pair of matching earrings that fell almost to her shoulders. Bracelets with each stone encased in fine wire cages of gold. A wide choker necklace of pearls with a great polished teardrop ruby at its centre…

There were bolts of every kind of cloth from which wedding clothes were to be made. Pointless to say that they would not be needed. She designed, and her girls made, seven exquisite wedding dresses in figured silks. Dresses in every conceivable colour with long baggy pants to be worn beneath them, edged in embroidery. Underwear. *Thaubs.*

And then, one morning, she rose to find Fayad's mother arranging a gold cap hung all around with threads of gold, fine as silk, as long as her hair, on a tall stand in the centre of all this treasure.

So far she had resisted the temptation to try on any of the jewels. They were so exotic, so unreal, that to Leila's consternation she treated them almost as a joke.

But this was different and, unable to stop herself, she reached out a hand to touch the delicate threads. 'What is it?' she asked.

'It is your bridal cap,' Leila said, almost swooning with excitement, 'to be worn when you receive visitors for the seven days after the Emir comes to make your marriage.'

Make their marriage.

There could be no mistaking what she meant by that.

'Not yet…'

Please not yet. It was too soon. She had so much more to

do. She did not want to leave Ras al Kawi. She did not want to leave him…

'It is time, Violet,' Fayad's mother said firmly.

'Does he say that?' she asked. If he did then there would be no question that it was time for her to go.

'He says he is too busy to discuss it, but his grandfather grows impatient, and since everything is ready—the house, the dowry—there need be no more delay.'

That would be the grandfather who was supposed to be on his last legs, but who, far from fading, seemed to have regained much of his strength in the last months.

'Which means?' she asked, hoping against hope that weddings took as long to organise in Ras al Kawi as they did in London. Months and months…

'We'll hold the *maksar* the day after tomorrow,' Fayad's mother replied. 'All the women will come to see the dowry, to feast.' She smiled. 'Then my son will come in the evening.'

To make her his wife.

Leila shivered with delighted anticipation.

Violet just shivered. 'I really need to talk to him about this, Sheikha.'

'He flew to Ras al Hajar this morning. He won't be back until midday tomorrow. But you don't have to worry about a thing. Everything is arranged. We will pamper you, and paint you with the wedding henna. Dress you, veil you.' She headed for the door, then turned back. 'He will expect you to resist him. Did you know this?'

'I knew.'

'Not much.' And she smiled. 'Just a token…' Then, 'I'll be back in an hour.'

Oh, the temptation. How easy it would be to just let it happen. Allow his mother to go ahead with her plans. Say nothing…

How would he be able to refuse?

Such a thought was unworthy of her. Unworthy of a man who had given her everything.

'I'm going to take a walk, Leila.'

'Now?' The girl was an unenthusiastic walker. 'But we need to begin…'

'An hour.' Little enough time. 'I just need some air.' She made herself smile. 'There's no need for you to come with me.'

'Oh, well. If you're sure?'

'I'm sure.' She wanted to take one last walk through the gardens, take the path above the palace to the place that Fayad had taken her, where she could see the whole of the city spread out below her.

A messenger met her at the door with an envelope, hand-delivered from Amira al Sayyid. She pushed it into the pocket of the jeans she wore beneath the *abaya* she'd thrown on to keep out the heat.

Her bodyguard half rose, but she waved him back into the shade. 'Stay, Yusuf. I'm not going far.'

She walked through the garden, through the gate that led to the home farm, with its fruit trees, vegetable gardens, its small herd of goats that provided milk for yoghurt and cheese. Up the steep path to the flat rock that provided a seat at the highest point.

She had no idea how long she'd been sitting there when a shadow cut off the sun. Yusuf, grown anxious? Or Leila, full of guilt?

Fayad had known and respected the Emir of Ras al Hajar since boyhood. The man was everything he aspired to. Cleaving to the best that was traditional in their way of life, but modern in outlook. And his English wife was not only mother to his sons, but stood beside him on the political stage, an advocate for women and an ambassador for her country.

Already Violet was filling that role in his own life. Full of ideas, proactive supporter of all his projects, in the task of convincing the conservative die-hards on the education question, talking to the women.

Every day he spent with her was a joy. And a day nearer the time she would leave Ras al Kawi and go back to her real life.

And every day he thought about the moment when she'd made him whole, when he'd cried out, "You are mine!" But he'd known even then that she would never belong to anyone. Only someone who was utterly free could have surrendered something as valuable as the Blood of Tariq and asked for nothing in return.

He'd known from the beginning that she had every quality that would make her a worthy queen. From the first moment he'd seen her, recognised her courage as she'd flown to her friend's aid, she'd overturned everything that was dead inside him.

The one thing he had not expected was to fall in love with her. It was something so new, so different. But this must be love, surely? Not just the derided western word for what was little more than lust, but the knowledge that grew stronger every day, that when she left him to return to her own life she would tear out his heart and take that, too.

He would give everything to have her by his side, his wife in every way.

'Fayad?' He realised that Hassan had asked him a question. Was waiting for an answer.

'I'm sorry…'

'Your mind is elsewhere. This will keep.' He stood, releasing him with a smile. 'Next time you come to Ras al Hajar, bring your new wife with you. Rose is eager to meet her.'

Before he could answer, he saw his aide coming towards him, his face white. Without a word, he handed him the cell-phone he was holding.

The caller did not bother introducing himself. All he said was, 'I have your wife.'

There was nothing else. No ransom demand. No threat.

There was no need.

He flew straight back to Ras al Kawi. Leila was distraught, blaming herself. 'She said she wanted to walk. To be alone.'

Violet's bodyguard was suicidal.

'Neither of you are to blame,' Fayad assured them. 'This is entirely my fault.'

He had brought her to Ras al Kawi. Worse, he had underestimated the ruthlessness of Ahmed al Sayyid and just how determined he was to get his hands on the dagger.

He drove alone to the place where he was to deliver the *khanjar*. He took no one with him, would not risk Violet's life by deviating from the instructions he'd been given. By attempting a rescue attempt.

He had been careless of his first wife, his son, and he had lost them. Now, when in his head he had offered all he had in return for the woman he loved, Allah had tested him, was calling on him to make good his word.

He left the four-wheel drive and, carrying the Blood of Tariq in one hand, walked towards the narrow bridge slung across a high gorge.

Ahmed al Sayyid stood at the far end of the bridge, holding Violet by the wrist. With a gesture he made the point that if there was one false move on his part he would pitch her into chasm.

He walked slowly towards them, making sure that his hands were always in sight, set the *khanjar* down at the centre of the bridge, then turned to walk back.

The tension was unbearable. Would she follow? Would they keep her until they had roused their supporters, deriding him as weak, unfit to lead their country? For the first time in his life he looked back. Straight into Violet's eyes, and said, so that all could hear him, not that foolish, possessive "you are mine", but stood as a man should and said, 'I am yours.'

'Go and pack your bags, Fayad al Kuwani,' Ahmed mocked. 'I'll send your wife to join you in exile in her little house in London.'

He'd looked back. That was all Violet could think as she was delivered to the small private jet. He'd looked back and said, 'I am yours.'

He had not just surrendered everything for her. He had surrendered himself.

The plane was in the air for only twenty minutes, and when it touched down the first person aboard was Fayad. No holding back, no distance. He gathered her in his arms, held her close. 'My heart…you are safe.' Then, looking at her. 'They did not hurt you?'

'I am safe,' she repeated, clinging to him despite every promise she'd made herself. 'I was so afraid for you.' They'd had guns, and it would have been the work of a moment to have killed him once they had what they wanted. Then, 'You just gave it up. Handed over the Blood of Tariq for me. Are you prepared to go into exile…?'

'Would you come with me?'

'To the ends of the earth…' Then, because that really left her completely exposed, with no hiding place, 'Where on earth are we?'

'Ras al Hajar. This aircraft belongs to Ahmed al Sayyid and the pilot is married to Amira al Sayyid. Amira, however, wants her girls to go to school, and so she told him that if he took you to London he need not come home.'

'I know Amira. She comes to the *majlis*. In fact…' She dug into her pocket, drew out the envelope that had been delivered earlier that day. 'She sent me this, this morning.' Tearing it open, she found a letter, written in Arabic. 'This is Fatima's letter,' she said. 'The one that was stolen from my house…'

Fayad skimmed it. Then grabbed her and kissed her. 'Ahmed may have the Blood of Tariq, but he does not have you, twin of my soul.'

Twin of his soul…? 'What does it say?'

'It's a confession. Written when she was old, near death. I believe she meant to send it to my great-great-grandfather, but maybe she left it too late.'

'Yes, but what does it say?'

'Her marriage to Tariq al Kuwani was arranged by her father for the sole purpose of stealing the *khanjar* from him. The plan was that she should drug him, take it, make her escape by night.'

Violet caught her breath. 'If she had been caught…'

'I know. Death would have been certain, but it was for her tribe, her family. Her brother was to wait for her at a given place every night until she escaped. It was weeks before she could bring herself to do it—would not have if her father hadn't made her swear on the holy Q'uran. When she finally forced herself to do it, her brother was not there. Perhaps he'd given up, or thought that she'd been caught and killed. She couldn't go back and, knowing that her husband would kill her if he found her, she ran.'

'And was found by my great-great-grandfather.'

'He saved her life, paid her passage to England—because he knew what would happen to her if he left her behind to fend for herself. Then he married her in England when he was discharged from the army.'

'He was a true hero, then.'

He took her hand. 'Not all Hamilton men are bad, Violet.'

She shook her head. 'No…'

'Fatima vowed to make the most of her second chance, vowed to be a good wife to him. Bought him the house with her gold.'

'But she hid the *khanjar*.'

'It was famous. If it had appeared in London…' He left her to imagine what would have happened.

'I don't think it was chance that Lawrence put that fancy bit of cutlery in your great-great-grandfather's hand,' she said. 'He chose wisely. And now, because of me, you have lost it.'

'You gave me everything you had and I could do no less for you.' She tried to speak but he stopped her. 'Later. My plane is waiting to take us back to Ras al Kawi.'

'Not exile, then?'

'The Kuwani have ruled Ras al Kawi for ninety years without your "fancy bit of cutlery", Violet. It takes more than a symbol to hold a country together over many generations, to bind it into a nation. It takes heart. Something that you have in abundance.' Then, 'Do you really want to go to London? Or does "the ends of the earth" include the bed of the Emir of Ras al Kawi, Violet Hamilton?' He took both her hands in his. 'You are my wife, the owner of my heart, the twin of my soul. Nothing will ever change that. Now I ask you, in your own language, in words that you will understand, will you stay at my side for always, be the mother of my children?'

Violet lifted her hand to his cheek. 'I will be at your side for always, Fayad al Kuwani, owner of my heart, twin of my soul. Be the mother of your sons, *insh'Allah*. Or your daughters, if that is his wish.'

And when their plane touched down in Ras al Kawi an hour later, Violet was not whisked away in a limousine while her husband was greeted by the tribal leaders. On this occasion she had her own reception, as the head of every *hareem*—with Amira al Sayyid first in line—waited to touch her hands, kiss her forehead, welcome her home.

The Sayyid coup was put down without bloodshed. Even those who had sided with Ahmed on the question of education were horrified at what he had done, and in their effort to distance themselves from him were swift to ally themselves with the Emir.

The *khanjar* was returned anonymously and Fayad wore it when he arrived at the *maksar*, three days later, to claim his bride.

In the silence of the bridal chamber, Violet waited for her husband. Her hands and feet had been painted with the ornate bridal patterns. Her friends, Leila and Amira and Fayad's mother, had, giggling like girls, wrapped her in a series of gauzy gold-edged veils.

Fayad met little resistance at the door as those who guarded Violet bowed him through, but his heart was in his mouth as he opened the last door, saw her waiting for him, gift-wrapped and sitting upon a white sheet.

He expected that she would fight him, just a little, but as he picked up the edge of the first veil, 'My love,' he said, his voice shaking just a little. 'Will you have me?'

'My lord…'

Her voice was shaking, too, he realised. She was trembling. It was not what he'd expected from his modern British bride. He'd expected giggles, a pretend fight…

He kissed the edge of the first veil and slowly removed it.

'I have to tell you something, keeper of my heart, twin of my soul. I have to tell you why, when my grandfather, my family, pressed me to marry I refused to consider it.'

She looked up and he kissed the edge of another veil and slowly removed it.

'The truth is that I was so racked with guilt at the death of my wife, my son, I was useless to a woman.

'But…'

He smiled as he removed yet another veil, could see her eyes widen with surprise. Well, of course she must have been aware of the effect that she had on him. When he had kissed her, had come within a hair's breadth of making their marriage a reality…

'It is because of you that I have my country. Because of you that I am a man…'

Another veil fell, revealing a hand. He lifted it, kissed each finger, turned it over to kiss the pad of her thumb, her palm.

There was no fight. Just a slow, sensuous unwrapping of his beautiful bride. He kissed every trembling inch of her until she was melting, imploring, begging for him to make their marriage complete. At which point he discovered that the white sheet was no mere symbol.

That Violet Hamilton had, indeed, given him everything.

* * * * *

Coming Next Month

Available April 12, 2011

#4231 THE BABY PROJECT
Susan Meier
Babies in the Boardroom

#4232 IN THE AUSTRALIAN BILLIONAIRE'S ARMS
Margaret Way

#4233 HOW TO LASSO A COWBOY
Shirley Jump
The Fun Factor

#4234 RICHES TO RAGS BRIDE
Myrna Mackenzie

#4235 RANCHER'S TWINS: MOM NEEDED
Barbara Hannay
Rugged Ranchers

#4236 FRIENDS TO FOREVER
Nikki Logan

HRCNM0311

Selene wanted nothing to do with the father of her son, Alex; but Aristedes had other plans…that included them.

Read on for an sneak peek from THE SARANTOS SECRET BABY by Olivia Gates, available April 2011, only from Harlequin Desire.

"You were right to turn my marriage offer down," Aristedes said.

And Selene found her voice at last, found the words that would not betray the blow he'd dealt her. "Thanks for letting me know. You didn't have to come all the way here, though. You could have just let it go. I left yesterday with the understanding that this case is closed."

Before the hot needles behind her eyes could dissolve into an unforgivable display of stupidity and weakness, she began to close the door.

The door stopped against an immovable object. His flat palm.

"I can't accept that." His voice was low, leashed.

What did her tormentor mean now? Was he ending one game only to start another?

She raised eyes as bruised as her self-respect to his, found nothing there but solemnity and determination.

Before she could voice her confusion, he elaborated. "I never let anything go unless I'm certain it's unworkable. I realize I made you an unworkable offer, and that's why I'm withdrawing it. I'm here to offer something else. A workability study."

She leaned against the door, thankful for its support and partial shield. "Your son and I are not a business venture you can test for feasibility."

His gaze grew deeper, made her feel as if he was trying to delve into her mind, take control of it. "It's actually the

SDEXP0411

other way around. I'm the one who would be tested."

She shook her head. "Why bother? I know—and *you* know—you're not workable. Not with me."

His spectacular eyebrows lowered over eyes she felt were emitting silver hypnosis. "You're right again. Neither you nor I have any reason to believe that isn't the truth. The only truth. It might be best for both you and Alex to never hear from me again, to forget I exist. But then again, maybe not. I'm only asking for the chance for both of us to find out for certain. You believe I'm unworkable in any personal relationship. I've lived my life based on that belief about myself. I never really had reason to question it. But I have one now. In fact, I have two."

Find out what happens in
THE SARANTOS SECRET BABY by Olivia Gates,
available April 2011, only from Harlequin Desire.

SDEXP0411

MARGARET WAY

In the Australian Billionaire's Arms

Handsome billionaire David Wainwright isn't about to let his favorite uncle be taken for all he's worth by mysterious and undeniably attractive florist Sonya Erickson.

But David soon discovers that Sonya's no greedy gold digger. And as sparks sizzle between them, will the rugged Australian embrace the secrets of her past so they can have a chance at a future together?

Don't miss this incredible new tale, available in April 2011 wherever books are sold!